GNOMES

Origin of the Species

IAN McBRIDE

Any reference to historical events, real people, or real places are used fictitiously. Names, characters, and places are products of the author's imagination.

Cover by: SWATT Books Ltd
Paintings by: Ian McBride
Typesetting by: SWATT Books Ltd

Printed in the United Kingdom
First Printing, 2022

ISBN: 978-1-7391812-0-8 (Paperback)
ISBN: 978-1-7391812-1-5 (eBook)

Ian McBride
Southampton, SO18 4FE

Dedicated to

my daughter Angela, who made the brown pottery Gnome Guard that has stood in my front garden for 35 years – which was probably the inspiration for this book.

Introduction

In a hidden valley in Switzerland (surrounded by mountains), is a land so secret that no human being had ever discovered it. It is a beautiful valley with fields and trees and flowers. A large lake is situated at one end of the valley, and on the edge of the lake at the foot of the mountains is a cluster of cottages. At the other end of the valley is a vast forest, and just before the forest is a much larger group of cottages. This larger quantity of cottages is in fact the town of Stonemarble and the small cluster is the village of Grassroot. Hang on a minute, I hear you remark. If the valley is so secret, why are there any cottages? Well, I'll tell you. This place is the Valley of Gnomes and it is the only place in the world where gnomes can exist without interference from humans.

The story I am about to tell relates to one particular family of gnomes. This family live in Grassroot. They used to live in Stonemarble, but moved to the village for a bit of peace and quiet. They live as a family much like humans do. The only difference being that gnomes live to an average age of about 350 years. All gnomes have strange sounding names, which are palindromic. That means that they read the same backwards as they do forwards. The reason for this is that gnomes have a spiral brain, and at times of stress they tend to talk backwards. Therefore, if they need to call the children in for tea and they are in backwards mode, the name still comes out the same.

There are five members of this family, they are Romanamor, the dad; Cramarc, the mum; and the three sons, Tippit, Pullup and Potstop. They live in a cottage at the top of the village. Also living with them, but in a self-contained annex at the side of the house, is Great Uncle Gnong. Gnomes tend to look after their old people very well and Great Uncle Gnong was nearly 280 years old, whereas Romanamor and Cramarc were relative youngsters at 160 and 152 respectively. The children were, in comparison to Great Uncle Gnong, really young. Tippit was the eldest at 54 years old, Pullup the second eldest was 47 years old and Potstop was the baby of the trio at 31 years old. As you know, time is a relative thing, and gnomes mature much more slowly than us humans. So, in human terms, Great Uncle Gnong was about 80, Romanamor, 46; Cramarc, 41; and the children were 16, 14 and 11 years old.

The family lived quite contentedly growing their own vegetables on a small plot of land behind the cottage. Gnomes are completely vegetarian and their favourite meal is cauliflower and parsnip stew, which they usually have as a special meal once a week. They also make carrot beer and whiskey, which the male folk consume in large quantities on Saturday nights in the large communal hut situated in the middle of the village.

As gnomes are a peace-loving race, all the arguments that may ensue as a result of the drinking are settled amicably. Although gnomes are fairly strong-minded beings, agreeing to differ seems to be their motto, and they usually keep their opinions to themselves.

In another large hut near the middle of the village, the female folk meet on Sunday nights where they consume large amounts of wine, which is fermented from all different kinds of vegetables and fruit.

This way the gnomes live in complete harmony with one another, the male and female folk both having their night out on the town, so to speak. The fact that they go out on different nights means that there is always someone at home to look after the children.

So, we can gather that the gnome community is a peace-loving one with happiness and harmony being the order of the day. However, unfortunately for every good side in life there has to be a bad one. And the bad side to the peaceful lives of the gnomes lives just over a small mountain range, on the right side of the valley. The bad side is a valley much smaller than the one where the gnomes live, but is far more densely populated by creatures, which were the complete opposite of gnomes. This is the Valley of the Elves.

Elves are mean, spiteful, nasty little creatures. In fact, one could imagine that the very word evil is derived from the word elves. They are ruled over by the Duke and Duchess of Pointstick, who have two sons Snitchmire and Prodlife, whose jobs are to make sure that the other elves stay evil and don't try and convert to niceness. Although there's not much chance of this, because elves have been evil for so many generations, that they would be miserable being any other way.

Elves are also very lazy, too lazy in fact to grow much food of their own. Why should they? When they could send raiding parties through the cave system (a maze of caves, which join the two lands) into Gnomeland and steal vegetables grown by the hard-working gnomes. Vegetables alone do not suffice, and the elves eat rats and squirrels as well, which they cook on sticks held over open fires. Sometimes they were too lazy to cook and they just ate the rats and squirrels raw. As you can see, the elves don't have to try too hard to make themselves as horrible as possible.

There is also a tunnel that runs under the big mountains connecting Gnomeland to Humanland. This tunnel is too small for humans to ever get through, but gnomes and elves, being small, can travel through quite easily. The gnomes are fairly timid beings and would never voluntarily venture into the tunnel. However, the elves being bolder and more aggressive, go through the tunnel quite frequently. Small bands of elves would often go through and steal food or anything that took their fancy from the human village nearest to the exit of the tunnel. So that the tunnel wouldn't be discovered, they had planted some very dense, prickly bushes in front of the exit, and sometimes at night, even the elves cannot find the way back in and wander for hours trying to find it.

Now, because the gnomes over the centuries have had to put up with aggressive elves coming through the tunnel and annoying them, they have developed a defence mechanism whereby they can turn solid in times of danger to prevent themselves being hurt. No one can explain how they can do this, but mother nature has devised her own ways of protecting the weak.

The elves at their most wicked, can turn anything to their own advantage and they realised many years ago, that maybe the creatures in Humanland would like and possibly buy these solid gnomes. The Duke and Duchesses' ancestors had solved the problem of trading the gnomes without having any contact with humans. They had realised that the humans did not all live together in the villages, some of the villagers lived alone. They were known as loners or outcasts and were looked upon by other humans as being a bit strange or simple.

Now the elves knew where a few of these simple humans lived and decided they could use them as go-betweens to sell the gnomes. The elves would leave the gnomes on the doorsteps of the outcasts with notes saying what was required in exchange for the gnomes. The outcasts would take the gnomes into the village and sell them. With the money, they would buy whatever was required and make a tidy profit in the bargain. Then they would leave whatever it was on their doorstop at night, in the morning another gnome would appear as if by magic. The humans in the villages thought that the simple ones were making the gnomes, and had no idea how they were really acquired, not that they worried about that too much, because gnomes soon became the garden accessory that no one could do without. They painted the gnomes bright red, so that everyone could see them and they put them in various positions in the garden. Some were sat by garden ponds with fishing rods, and others were given spades, forks, trowels, or even miniature wheelbarrows – anything that would make their gnomes different from anyone else's.

Humans also like making money and they soon realised that they could reproduce the gnomes in a factory and sell them to other countries. So now we have gnomes all over the world, but the originals stayed in Switzerland. No matter how hard they tried, the humans could never make their gnomes as life-like as the ones they bought from the elves.

Chapter 1

Potstop is Missing

So, this nasty little trade went on, and over the years the elves got greedy and more and more gnomes were disappearing from Gnomeland. Now, the gnomes do not have rulers like the Duke and Duchess of Pointstick, but they do have a council made up of the oldest and the wisest gnomes, that only ever meet up in the times of severe crisis. Great Uncle Gnong was one of the council members, but up until now he had not realised how desperate the situation had become, regarding the kidnappings of the young gnomes. He was sat under an apple tree in the vegetable garden one sunny morning, contentedly smoking his cherrywood pipe, when Cramarc came rushing into the garden.

"Whatever is the matter?" Said Gnong.

"Potstop is missing! Have you seen him anywhere? I haven't seen him since he went to bed last night, and when I went to look for him this morning, there were ruffled blankets and an empty bed."

"No, I'm afraid I haven't," replied Gnong looking seriously worried.

"Do Tippit and Pullup know where he is?"

"Of course they don't, if they did, they would have told me," said Cramarc tearfully.

Gnong looked at the ground, then up into the apple tree, then at some distant point on the horizon, until finally his woeful gaze rested on Cramarc. She looked straight back into his eyes and as if reading each other's minds "SEVLE!" they shouted, going into backwards mode simultaneously.

"Eht sevle evah deppandik Potstop!!"

"Ho ym," sobbed Cramarc. "Tahw era ew gniog ot od?"

Gnong shook his head rapidly up and down to try and get his brain thinking forwards again. Finally he said, "I think the time has come to call a meeting of the elders."

"Tahw doog lliw taht od?" Asked Cramarc.

"I don't know," replied Gnong. "But it's what we gnomes always do in times of crisis."

"Etsaw fo emit," sobbed Cramarc. "Ydobon sah reve neeb elba ot od gnihtyna tuoba eht sevle."

Just then Romanamor, Tippit and Pullup came into the garden, they had been working on one of the large communal vegetable plots since dawn and had now returned for some breakfast. Potstop, being the youngest didn't have to go, therefore his absence had not been noticed. Gnong explained what had happened, because Cramarc was still in serious backwards mode and was not making any sense. Romanamor by sheer strength of willpower managed to keep himself forwards, but Tippit and Pullup both got very upset.

"Roop roop Potstop!!" Exclaimed Tippit tearfully. "Woh emoc ew reven draeh eht sevle emoc ni?"

Romanamor explained that elves were the sneakiest, quietest creatures imaginable when they wanted to be, and that once Potstop had solidified, there was no possibility of him crying for help. Pullup didn't go into backwards mode or forwards mode, he just stood there totally shocked, in no mode at all.

Gnong told them of his planned meeting of the elders, and Romanamor suggested that when everyone had calmed down, they should have a family meeting to discuss what Gnong was going to say. So a little while later when everyone was speaking forwards again, they sat around the big oak table in the kitchen and began to discuss what they ought to do.

They talked round in circles for a long time and still didn't reach any decisions. Romanamor had not joined in the discussion, but had sat there with a deep frown on his face, getting more and more angry about the situation. Finally he spoke.

"I think we ought to try and get Potstop back," he announced.

"Tahw?" Said everyone else, temporarily going into backwards mode.

No gnome had ever ventured into the tunnel. Had Romanamor gone mad?

"Have you gone mad?" Asked Cramarc.

"We can do it," said Romanamor. "We must find the courage from somewhere to try and get Potstop back!"

"But gnomes are traditionally cowards," said Cramarc. "We'll never be brave enough, and what if we get scared? We would turn solid in the middle of a strange land, never to be heard of again. That's what!"

"And if we don't get scared, we have a chance of getting him back," answered Romanamor.

"We're with Dad," said Tippit.

Pullup agreed. "Yes, life's going to be very dull without Potstop around."

"Okay," said Cramarc. "Maybe we ought to try and do something, but first we must see what the elders have to say."

Gnong agreed. "Unfortunately," he said, "The elders don't allow other gnomes to attend their meetings, but I will put your plans forward to them on your behalf."

Gnong arranged the meeting for the next morning. The elders gathered around in the communal hut and Gnong explained that the family had decided to do something about Potstop's disappearance.

"They're crazy," said the elders in unison.

"You're right," said Gnong. "But the rest of the family are insisting on doing something to save Potstop."

Garfrag, Sullus, Barrab, Wollow and Martram just sat there thinking. Whereas the chairman of the council, Corabaroc paced up and down the hut. He was also thinking, trying to drag up a memory from the distant past. A memory that involved a family long ago who made an expedition into Humanland, one member came back, Frogorf was his name. Frogorf was so ashamed about losing the rest of his family, that he had gone to live in the caves beyond the Grey Wood. He lived in isolation and had never dared show his face to other gnomes since.

Corabaroc related this story to Gnong and the rest of the council.

"Doesn't exactly encourage anyone to follow in their footsteps," said Garfrag.

"You wouldn't catch one of us doing it," said Wollow. "The whole idea is quite insane."

Corabaroc tried to plunge deeper into his memory. He sat for a long, long time, a huge frown on his face, trying to recall more about the tale of Frogorf. Finally he spoke, "I seem to recall that Frogorf had made a vow that no family should ever again be put in the same position as the one he lost. He also vowed that he would spend the rest of his days trying to develop a potion that would give gnomes courage, so that they would not go solid when under threat. Unfortunately no one knows if he is still alive, let alone if he succeeded in developing such a potion."

Corabaroc sat down and held his head in his hands. Gnomes are not known for making long speeches and this was probably the longest speech a Gnome had made for a very long time.

Gnong considered what Corabaroc had said. "Well, if this Frogorf fellow is still alive and if he has developed a potion, then we must go and see him."

So the council meeting was reaching the end, but first, as with all council meetings, they must have a vote.

"Do we all agree that if the family decide to go, we will give them all the help that we can?" Said Corabaroc. "All those in favour say, aye."

"Aye," said all the gnomes together.

"Motion carried," said Corabaroc. "I'd like to close the meeting by wishing Gnong's family lots of luck, because I think they are going to need it."

So the gnome elders went back to their cottages, and within hours every gnome in the village was gossiping and speculating about the brave family who had decided (against most of the gnomes' better judgement), to embark on the journey to Humanland.

Gnong returned back home.

"Well?" Asked Romanamor. "What did the council think?"

Gnong explained what the council had thought and then went on to relay the story of Frogorf the hermit and the fact that there was maybe a potion they could use to help them in their quest.

"This is good news," enthused Cramarc. "We must go as soon as possible and try to find Frogorf."

Romanamor thought for a while, in the way that male gnomes do. Picking his words carefully, so as not to upset anyone, he said, "I think it might be an idea if some of us stayed here to look after our vegetable plot, because it is going to be left for long enough, unattended if we go to Humanland."

Cramarc agreed. Romanamor suggested that he and Tippit, the eldest son should go. Leaving Cramarc, Pullup and Gnong to look after the vegetable plot and the cottage.

Chapter 2

In Search of Frogorf

Now gnomes do not really like going on long journeys, because their short, stubby legs make it difficult for them to move faster than a slow walking pace. They had estimated that it would take three days to reach the cave at the other side of the Grey Wood. Cramarc packed six days' worth of fruit and vegetables, some blankets and a change of clothes for each of her loved ones. Also a large flagon of fresh water, and because Romanamor would miss out on his Saturday night with the other male gnomes, she packed a small flagon of carrot whiskey. And so it was that with many tears and goodbye pecks on the cheek, Romanamor and Tippit set off in search of Frogorf the hermit.

All the neighbours and friends turned out to see them off and wish them luck. All through that first day, every gnome that they passed wished them well in their quest. Some gave them gifts of more vegetables, and one really nice couple, who lived on the outskirts of gnome territory, offered them shelter for the night plus some large helpings of home-made apple pie and a few glasses of carrot beer. Now, Romanamor had never heard of

Tromort and Agninga (the couple who gave them shelter), but they had heard of him, for by now news of the family's planned adventure had spread throughout Gnomeland. Tromort told Romanamor and Tippit that he and his wife had also lost a son to the elves and knew exactly how he was feeling. He also said that what the family was planning to do had given a faint glimmer of hope to all gnomes whose children had been kidnapped.

"Who knows?" He said, "If you are successful, we too in future times may be able to recover Naggan, our son."

Agninga looked tearfully at Tromort. "Our lives are so empty now Naggan has gone, why don't you accompany them to Humanland?"

Tromort put his arm around his wife. "We must be patient, dear, I don't know if I can find the courage for such a trip."

Romanamor relayed to Tromort and Agninga the story of Frogorf and the potion.

Romanamor thought for a while. "I'll tell you what we'll do," he said. "If we find Frogorf and if he has developed a potion, then we will call in to see you on our return and then you can decide whether you wish to come with us."

So it was agreed that if the potion was found, they would come back and Tromort could then decide if he wanted to go to Humanland.

It was now early morning and a mist was spreading over the heathland up towards the Grey Wood. Another two-day journey lay ahead for Romanamor and Tippit, and they wanted to leave early to make the most of the daylight hours. So they said their farewells and set off at a reasonably fast pace towards the Grey Wood. Now, the territory that they were entering was rarely visited by gnomes, and there was no trail to follow like there is in the rest of Gnomeland. But gnomes over the years have developed an uncanny sense of direction, they just think about where they want to go and their legs just follow where they are thinking. Mother Nature had been good to them in this respect, because only a few hundred years ago a gnome could get lost just travelling a hundred yards, but now they can travel for miles using their sixth sense as a guide. The fact that they knew they would get to where they were going didn't mean they weren't scared, and Tippit followed very closely in his father's footsteps. So closely in fact, that when his father stopped occasionally to take a breather, Tippit would bump into him. Romanamor got a bit fed up with this, and eventually made Tippit walk alongside him, giving him as he did so, words of assurance that nothing bad was going to happen, and wishing at the same time that he could believe the words he was saying.

The mist was now clearing and Romanamor and Tippit began to feel more cheerful.

"I think that we should be on the edge of the Grey Wood before nightfall," said Romanamor.

"That's good," said Tippit. "So long as we wait till daylight before going into the wood."

"Don't worry your little gnome head about that," replied Romanamor.

"Even I would not enter the Grey Wood at night-time."

So they trudged on at a gnomely pace, not saying much to each other because they needed all their energy just to keep moving. The route they were travelling on seemed to become steeper towards the end of the morning, and the pace of the gnomes slowed accordingly. By midday they were both ready for a good rest and some food. They found a little grassy alcove behind some rocks where they decided to rest for a while.

They looked back on the valley that was their home.

"How beautiful it looks from up here", said Romanamor.

Tippit gazed misty-eyed at the view. "It might look beautiful from up here, but I wish we were down there and Potstop had never been taken by those wicked elves."

"So do I," admitted Romanamor. "I wish that elves didn't exist at all, but the fact remains that they do, and we will have to try our utmost to get Potstop back."

So Romanamor and Tippit just sat in peace for a while quietly munching on some of the vegetables they had bought with them. They refilled their flagons from a nearby mountain stream and took long swigs of the cool, refreshing water before they decided that it was time to make a move.

"My legs are aching," moaned Tippit. "I'm not used to this much exercise."

"So are mine," agreed his father. "Us gnomes are not used to walking such long distances, but the best cure for aching legs is to keep them moving and try to forget about the pain."

"All right," said Tippit. "I'll try, I know we have to keep going if we want to reach the Grey Wood by nightfall."

So off they trudged, uphill all the way, and the hill was getting steeper by the minute. In the distance they could see the tree-tops of Grey Wood, which as they walked, were very gradually becoming closer. Towards the end of the afternoon, they stopped for a short while on the banks of a mountain stream. Romanamor bent his head forward and plunged it into the cool water. Tippit followed his father's example, but being shorter than his father, over-balanced and toppled into the stream. Tippit being rather quick minded for a gnome, immediately made out that he had dived in deliberately, saying how refreshing it was to be completely immersed in the water, not mentioning however, the fact that it was only luck that the stream was shallow enough for a small gnome to stand in and keep his head above water.

His father smiled knowingly. "Time we were going," he said, reaching out with his arms and pulling Tippit out of the water.

So they set off again, moving faster now, revitalised by the effects of the stream water. The Grey Wood and the darkness of the night grew nearer at the same time and an evening mist was beginning to form over the heathland.

"It's about time we looked for a suitable spot to stop for the night," said Romanamor. "We don't want to be too close to the woods at night, just in case."

"Just in case of what?" Said Tippit, beginning to feel a bit frightened.

"Err... not in case of anything much," lied Romanamor. "But with all those trees in the way, we are more likely to find somewhere we can lay down before we get to the wood."

"Yes Dad," said Tippit, relieved that they weren't going any further. "It will be nice to settle down for the night. You know what? I'm absolutely exhausted."

"Over there looks a good place to spend the night," said his father.

"I'm so tired I could sleep on a bed of pine needles," yawned Tippit.

So they settled down, snuggled under the warm blankets that they had brought from Grassroot. Soon they were fast asleep, snoring contentedly and loudly, for there is one thing that gnomes should be famous for, it's loud snoring. And they snored and snored until morning. In fact they snored and snored until halfway through the morning, and then it was only the fact that a large fly had landed on Tippit's nose and made him sneeze that they awoke. The sun was already high in the sky, the dawn chorus had finished hours ago, and Romanamor and Tippit, who were usually up with the sunrise, realised they had wasted good travelling time, and needed to be on their way as soon as possible. They quickly ate their breakfast, which consisted of potato and broccoli pie, followed by an apple, and packed up their belongings and set off in the direction of the Grey Wood.

The wood was called the Grey Wood because it was very dense and therefore very dark and foreboding. Romanamor and Tippit had to summon up every ounce of courage that gnomes possess (which as you know isn't very much), before they could actually enter the wood.

"Can't we just klaw round eht edistuo?" Asked Tippit slipping slightly into backwards mode.

"Too far," said Romanamor. "We must follow the shortest route if we are to be back home in six days."

"Yako," said Tippit. "I will yrt and eb evarb."

So our intrepid travellers entered the outskirts of the Grey Wood. Once inside the woods, they realised it wasn't as scary as they had thought.

In fact it was rather calm and peaceful, the only sounds being the birds high up in the treetops and the scampering, rustling sounds of the occasional squirrel, frantically running away from these intruders. The crunching noise the gnomes made as they walked along the bracken covered floor, was in fact the loudest noise in the wood.

Slowly, they picked their way through the trees, stopping occasionally to pick some of the wild strawberries that grew on the forest floor. It seemed to the gnomes that they had been walking through the wood forever, when it was actually only a few hours. They had luckily chosen the narrowest part of the wood to travel through and they could just make out bright sunlight glimmering through the trees in the distance.

"Nearly there," said Romanamor.

“Thank goodness for that,” said Tippit. “My legs are beginning to ache.”

“Still, the journey back should be much quicker as we will be able to follow our own footsteps,” said Romanamor.

“Does that mean we have to walk backwards?” Asked Tippit.

“Of course not, you silly gnome. I don't mean we actually fit our feet in our footsteps, just that we can use them as a guide to get us back.”

“Of course, silly me, I really am quite daft sometimes, aren't I?” Said Tippit.

“Not daft son, just young with a lot to learn,” replied Romanamor understandingly.

Finally they reached the other side of the wood and emerged, blinking into the bright sunlight. It took a while for their eyes to become accustomed to the light after being in the darkness of the Grey Wood for most of the day. They walked to the top of the heather-covered ridge beyond the wood. The vista that beheld their gaze was quite the most incredible sight they had ever seen. There was row upon row of small statues of gnomes. The rows disappeared into a small valley and the statues stood like sentries on either side of it. From the other end, a plume of smoke was rising and Romanamor and Tippit could hear a faint chinking sound, much the same noise as builders in Stonemarble would make when building a new cottage.

“What do we do now?” Asked Tippit tentatively.

"Well, we have come this far, we may as well investigate what exactly is going on here," said Romanamor.

So they set off down the valley towards the plume of smoke and the chinking sound. As they walked, they saw that even more of the stone gnomes were placed up the sides of the valley. The whole place looked like some sort of monument to Gnomeland. The chinking sound stopped and a kind of eerie silence fell on the valley. Romanamor shivered slightly as the whole atmosphere in the valley changed. There was a kind of intimidating, menacing feel to the valley now that Romanamor didn't like.

"And who might you be?" Came a booming voice from behind one of the larger stone statues.

"Romanamor and Tippit," said Romanamor shakily. "We have come from Grassroot to try and find Frogorf the hermit."

"Never heard of him!" Boomed the voice.

Tippit was hidden behind his father trying his best not to turn into one of the stone statues.

"Well, we've heard of him and we heard he lived up here above the Grey Forest," answered Romanamor.

"Lies, lies," came the reply. "You've been told a whole pack of lies."

"Why don't you come out from behind that statue?" Asked Romanamor.

"Because I don't exist!" Came the answer.

"If you don't exist how come you're talking?" Said Romanamor.

"Figment of your imagination matey, you've been drinking too much carrot whiskey!" The voice replied.

"Well, if you don't come out, we're coming up there!" Romanamor said, getting slightly annoyed.

Slowly, a figure emerged from behind the statue, and there stood the largest gnome that Romanamor and Tippit had ever seen. Not large in the way that he was taller or wider than any other gnome, but large in a muscular kind of way. His arms were twice the thickness of other gnomes and his upper body bulged with muscle. Obviously all the years of building stone statues had built his body up into some sort of super gnome.

"Are you Frogorf the hermit?" Asked Romanamor.

"Is who Frogorf the what?" Boomed the big gnome aggressively.

"As far as we know, the only gnome living up here is Frogorf," said Romanamor.

"Well Frogorf doesn't exist anymore, he was a cowardly gnome who left his family all alone and solid in Humanland."

"So who are you?" Asked Tippit.

"I'm nobody," replied the gnome, with a slight tinge of sadness in his voice.

Romanamor decided to change his angle of approach.

"Would you like to share some food and carrot whiskey with us?" He asked.

"Carrot whiskey? You've got carrot whiskey? I haven't tasted that nectar of the gnomes for 180 years."

"Well come on then," said Romanamor. "We can you use your fire to make some cauliflower and parsnip stew."

"Cauliflower and parsnip stew, eh? Sounds lovely, all I grow are cabbages and broccoli, because that's the only seeds I had when I came up here."

"You mean all you've had to eat for 180 years is cabbages and broccoli? How boring," said Romanamor.

"Plus a few wild mushrooms and strawberries," said the gnome, trying his best to make wild mushrooms and strawberries interesting.

So Romanamor set about preparing the stew, remembering, as Cramarc had shown him, to throw in a large handful of mixed herbs to give the stew that extra special gnomish flavour.

Finally he said, "Okay it's ready to go on the fire now."

So the large gnome put the ingredients into one of his stone pots and placed it on the fire.

Tippit meanwhile had got bored and decided to go rock climbing up behind the cave, not that gnomes were really cut out for rock climbing, but he was fine so long as he only picked small rocks to climb on.

Romanamor sat down on a stone stool outside the cave entrance and from his bag produced the flagon of carrot whiskey. The large gnome produced two stone mugs and Romanamor poured some of the carrot whiskey into each. The large gnome sat for a while, holding the mug of carrot whiskey under his nose. A kind of smile spread over his face and distant memories flickered through his gnomish brain. As he sipped the whiskey, all the memories that he had pushed to one side for so long began to trickle back. He had lived alone with his guilt for too long, and now was maybe the time to ease his conscience.

"Yes," he said finally. "I am indeed Frogorf, and despite how hard I try, I cannot blank him out completely from my mind."

"Is it true that you actually went into Humanland?" Asked Romanamor.

"Yes, it is true, we went to look for our son. There were four of us, myself, my wife and my other son and daughter," he said tearfully.

"So what happened to the others?" Asked Romanamor.

"Well, the elves had followed us into Humanland and late one night, while we were resting, they surrounded us. I managed to run and hide in one of the human cottages, but alas, my wife and children weren't so lucky, and the elves took them away into the night."

By now the large gnome was crying openly into his carrot whiskey.

"So, did you make any effort to get them back?" Asked Romanamor.

"I'm afraid I was too much of a coward. I just stayed hidden for a couple of days and then hurried back to the tunnel as fast as I could. When I got back to Gnomeland I was so ashamed about what I had done that I couldn't face any other gnomes."

He took a large swig of his whiskey.

"You're the first gnome I've spoken to in 180 years."

"Are you making all the stone gnomes so that you don't feel so lonely?" Romanamor enquired.

"It may look that way," said Frogorf. "But actually, I'm paranoid about being taken by the elves, and if they do come, maybe they'll be happy just taking some of the statues and leave me alone."

"But why so many?" Asked Romanamor.

"I suppose it's just a habit, I just can't seem to stop making them," he said, flexing his huge arms as if he wanted to get back to his hammer and chisel.

"The other thing we heard is that you vowed to produce a potion that would give gnomes courage when they were in danger," quizzed Romanamor.

"Aha," said Frogorf. "I knew there was a real reason for you coming all the way up here just to see me."

Romanamor then explained the reason for his journey and that if such a potion existed, it would be very helpful to them in their quest to find his son.

"Oh I see," said Frogorf. "But if you take my advice, you wouldn't even be thinking about such a journey."

'Well I'm not here to seek your advice. I'm here to find out if you have concocted a potion," said Romanamor, getting slightly irritated by Frogorf's patronising manner.

"Okay, okay," said Frogorf. "I have tried to produce such a potion, and to some extent I think I have succeeded, but with only me to try it on, I don't really know if it works or not."

"What is it you've used to make this potion?" Asked Romanamor.

Frogorf went to the back of the cave and came back carrying a large flagon. Romanamor peered inside at what appeared to be some kind of grey soup.

"So that's it, is it?" He said.

"It's the best I could come up with, as you may have noticed, there aren't too many potential ingredients round here," said Frogorf defensively. "I experimented with various ingredients, but the only thing that had any effect were these mushrooms I found in the Grey Forest."

All of a sudden there was a loud backward cry for help, it came from the rocks behind the cave.

"Pleeeeh!!" Went the loud cry and there was silence.

"Ho ym ssendoog!" Exclaimed Romanamor. "S'gnihtemos deneppah ot Tippit."

"Oh, that's wonderful," said Frogorf. "Hearing backward speech after all these years certainly brings back memories."

"Reven dnim taht," shouted Romanamor, shaking his head violently to get his brain working forwards again. "Tippit si ni emos....kind of trouble."

"Sorry," apologised Frogorf. "I didn't mean to sound flippant, of course we must go immediately and find out what has happened."

So they hurried off to the place where Tippit had started his rock climbing and scrambled over the rocks as fast as their gnomish little legs could carry them. Up they went until they were at least 20 feet above the ground, which was pretty high for a gnome.

There was no sign of Tippit, so they climbed even higher and there, on a ledge as solid as the rocks they had been climbing on, lay Tippit. He had fallen from some rocks higher up and was so scared, as he fell, the *turn solid when in danger* mechanism kicked in, and by the time he had reached the ground, he'd become solid. Romanamor went over to pick him up with Frogorf following close behind.

"Ho raed, oh dear," stammered Romanamor. "Poor Tippit, I warned him about the dangers of being too adventurous."

"Would you like me to carry him?" Asked Frogorf, flexing his giant arms.

“Thanks,” said Romanamor. “He is getting a bit heavy for me to pick up nowadays and now he’s solid, he’ll be even heavier.”

So Frogorf gently picked up Tippit and laid him across one of his massive shoulders. Slowly they clambered their way back down to the cave. When they got there, Frogorf laid Tippit down on his makeshift mattress just inside the cave’s entrance.

“He doesn’t look any different,” said Romanamor sadly. “A little paler perhaps, apart from that, he still looks just the same.”

Frogorf was staring at Tippit, thinking of his own family and what had happened to them. He stared and thought for a long time, and as he stared and thought, an idea began to formulate in his mind.

“What if we were to give Tippit some of my potion?” He asked.

“Well, I don’t know,” said Romanamor. “What if it has the wrong kind of effect on him?”

“What could be more wrong than being solid? Let’s face it Romanamor, we’ve got nothing to lose.”

“Well, I suppose we could just try the tiniest amount and see what happens,” said Romanamor.

So Frogorf dipped his finger into the murky grey liquid and then held his finger over Tippit’s mouth so that the potion dripped onto Tippit’s lips. Then he withdrew his finger. He did not wish the recumbent gnome to have too much of the potion, because he wasn’t sure what effect it would have. The drops that had landed on Tippit's mouth just sat there for a while, and then slowly seeped through the tiny gap between his lips.

"We must give it a chance to start working," said Frogorf.

Romanamor was silent just watching his son for any signs of recovery.

"Could take hours," said Frogorf, beginning to doubt if the potion would work at all.

Romanamor sent a silent prayer up to the Great Gnome, who nobody believed in but everybody prayed to in times of trouble.

"Have faith in the potion," whispered a small voice somewhere inside of Romanamor's head. "Have faith in the potion, and your little one will be all right," repeated the voice.

As the voice faded, Tippit's body began to move. At first it was just his chest moving up and down very gradually. Then his arms stretched out as though he was waking up after a long sleep, and then suddenly, he sat bolt upright and began looking frantically round.

"Erehw ma I?" He exclaimed, looking startled.

"It's all right son, you're quite safe," said Romanamor.

Romanamor explained to Tippit what had happened. Tippit rocked his head backwards and forwards to correct his backwards mode.

"I'll never go rock climbing again," he said. "It's far too dangerous."

“You're right,” said Romanamor. “It's far too dangerous.” Whilst thinking secretly that the task they were about to undertake was far more dangerous than any rock climbing.

Frogorf meanwhile just stood there with a huge beaming smile on his face.

“Yes! Yes! Yes!” He kept saying. “The potion works, I've got the formula right and the potion actually works!”

Romanamor had been so relieved at Tippit's recovery, that the full significance of what had happened hadn't yet sunk in. Finally it did.

“Wow! My goodness! Fantastic!” He exclaimed. “Absolutely tremendous! Brilliant!” He carried on like his until he had finally run out of adjectives to describe the miracle that had occurred.

“This is the best thing that's ever happened in the lives of us gnomes, ever!” He said excitedly. “Finally there is hope that we may recover our lost children.”

“At last,” said Frogorf. “Maybe I can make amends for what I did all those years ago.”

“How much of the potion have you actually made?” Enquired Romanamor.

“Follow me,” said Frogorf.

They followed Frogorf to the back of the cave, and here, lined up along the back wall, were at least a dozen flagons of the potion.

"It took me longer to make the stone flagons than it did to make the potion," said Frogorf proudly.

"Quite an achievement," agreed Romanamor.

"And now to try some of your achievement," said Frogorf, looking hungrily towards the stew pot.

"You're welcome," said Romanamor. "It's the least we can offer you."

Frogorf only had one bowl, but he had plenty of spoons, so they decided to eat it straight from the pot. Frogorf had a huge appetite and managed to eat most of the stew all on his own.

"Magnificent," he said afterwards. "Best meal I've ever had."

And probably the smallest meal we've ever had, thought Romanamor to himself. The stew all gone; they began working out the best way of carrying the potion back to Grassroot.

"We can't carry all those flagons back," moaned Tippit. "They're far too heavy."

"I don't think you'll need all of them," said Frogorf. "In any case I need some here for my own use."

"I think I may be able to carry two flagons and maybe Tippit can carry one." Romanamor concluded.

Frogorf looked thoughtful. "I would help, but I don't really wish to go back to Gnomeland."

"Maybe you could carry some flagons part of the way, and then make your way back," said Romanamor.

"Mmmm," thought Frogorf. "Well I wouldn't want to go too far away from here," he said.

Tippit came up with an idea. "If you can help us carry as many flagons as possible to the other side of the Grey Forest. We can hide them and send other gnomes up for them later."

"Excellent idea, what do you think?" Romanamor asked Frogorf.

"I agree," said Frogorf. "I owe it to gnomekind to give you the best chance possible of success."

So they made ready for the journey, for not only did they have to carry the flagons of potion, but also food and drink supplies as well. Frogorf somehow had managed to pick up two of the flagons in each hand, Romanamor could carry two and Tippit one. It was late evening by the time they set off and they reached the Grey Wood just as it was beginning to get dark.

"I think we should rest here for the night," sighed Romanamor wearily.

"Good idea," said Frogorf. "Poor old Tippit looks absolutely exhausted."

"Yes, he does," agreed Romanamor, bravely trying to cover up the fact that he was just as exhausted as Tippit.

So they found what they thought would be a comfortable spot and settled down for the night, or in Romanamor and Tippit's case, collapsed for the night. Within a few minutes they were snoring away as only gnomes can.

Darkness fell and the gnomes snored on. Suddenly Frogorf woke with a start. "Elves! Elves!" He shouted, waking up the other two in the process.

"Where? Where?" Stammered Romanamor.

"Over there in the woods," said Frogorf.

"What are the elves doing up here?" Asked Romanamor.

"Ssh! Listen," whispered Frogorf.

So they kept quiet and listened. Sure enough there was a rustling sound and the sound of twigs breaking, as if someone or something was skulking around in the woods.

"Could be a deer," said Tippit hopefully.

"Yes, I expect that's what it is," answered Romanamor equally hopefully. But as they listened, a low cackling laugh emitted from the woods.

"Deer, my foot!" Said Frogorf "That's elves that is. I should know, they've been stalking me for as long as I can remember."

"But why?" Queried Romanamor.

"Spies!" Said Frogorf. "Sent up here because the elves want to keep an eye on what I'm doing."

"Will they attack?" Asked Tippit shakily.

"No," answered Frogorf. "They won't attack because they only send a couple of elves up here at a time, and they are only brave in numbers, in fact, they are probably more scared of us than we are of them".

"I don't believe that elves could be scared of anyone," said Romanamor.

"Well they're scared of me!" Said Frogorf. "Watch!"

So Romanamor and Tippit watched. Frogorf stood up and began running in the direction of the woods. Anyone seeing this huge muscular gnome running towards them would have been terrified, and the elves were no exception.

The sound that had been a low cackle changed to a higher pitch, and the elves ran off shrieking, back through the woods. There was an occasional cry of "Ouch" as they ran into trees in the darkness, and the occasional elf swear word as they tripped over tree roots. The sounds continued for a while, getting slowly fainter until they finally disappeared, along with the elves into the night.

Frogorf turned round and walked back to the others grinning from ear to ear.

"There you are. I told you they were scared stiff of me."

"But if they're so scared, why are you so paranoid about them coming to get you?" Asked Romanamor.

"Because if they come to get me, there will be a lot more than two. There may even be hundreds and even I couldn't overcome that many and the worst of it is they could come at any time." Explained Frogorf.

By the time the episode with the elves was over, it was too late to really make it worthwhile going back to sleep. Romanamor reached into the bag and pulled out three large apples and some broccoli, a combination very popular with gnomes, and they just sat there munching and talking until daybreak. When daylight came, Frogorf, who was always full of energy, was ready to be off.

"Come on." He said. "The sooner we go, the sooner we'll get there."

Romanamor and Tippit were still aching from the effort of carrying the flagons of potion the day before and were a little bit reluctant to move again.

"Come on, hurry up! Those elves I scared off may come back with a few of their friends," said Frogorf anxiously.

So Romanamor and Tippit dragged themselves to their feet, picked up their respective loads and started trudging towards the Grey Wood. Once they were in the wood, it became easier, because it was all downhill and they reached the other side by mid-day.

"Oh well, this is where we must part company," said Frogorf. "I'll just put these flagons here and be off then."

"What's the hurry?" Asked Romanamor.

"I must get back to my cave in case the elves return," said Frogorf, starting to get panicky.

"And I suppose we must be making tracks as well," agreed Romanamor,

"Are you sure you won't come with us? I'm sure the family would love to meet you."

"Thanks for asking," said Frogorf. "Maybe some time in the future I may come and see you, anyway, must go now, good luck in your search for Potstop."

Romanamor held out his hand, Frogorf shook it vigorously then shook Tippit's hand, but not anywhere near as hard.

"Good luck once again! You'll need it!" Said Frogorf. Then he turned and hurried back through the woods.

For a long while Romanamor and Tippit just stood there, slightly saddened by the fact that they were once again alone. The sounds of the giant gnome crashing his way through the undergrowth grew fainter and fainter, until they disappeared altogether.

"What a gnome!" Exclaimed Tippit.

"Yes," agreed Romanamor. "I wish he was coming with us."

"Still, look on the bright side Dad, at least we've got the potion."

"True," agreed Romanamor, a wide grin appearing on his face. "We've got the potion, the future is beginning to look brighter and I reckon we've got a damn good chance of getting Potstop back."

"Oh I do hope so Dad, I do hope so."

Chapter 3

Return and Preparation for the Journey

So our intrepid adventurers made ready for the next stage of their homeward journey. They hid the flagons of potion that Frogorf had carried, put on their rucksacks containing food and water, picked up the flagons they were taking with them and set off towards Grassroot.

From here it was all downhill and despite the extra weight they were carrying, they made reasonably fast progress and were almost at Tromort's house before darkness fell.

After the episode with the elves on the previous night, they needed to find somewhere secluded to rest, otherwise neither of them would get a wink of sleep. They found a rocky overhang hidden by some bushes.

"Perfect," said Romanamor. "We should be able to rest here without being disturbed."

"I'm glad about that," said Tippit. "My legs are completely worn out."

They had some supper and settled down for the night. Within a few minutes their loud snoring was the only thing to be heard. The trouble was, that no matter how well they hid themselves, their snoring could give them away. The gnomes did not realise this because gnomes, just like humans, always deny the fact that they snore when they're asleep.

Still, despite the snoring, the night passed without incident and Romanamor and Tippit awoke refreshed the next morning, ready to continue their journey.

"Should be there by lunchtime," said Romanamor, hoisting his rucksack onto his back.

"The sooner we get back to civilisation, the happier I'll be," said Tippit.

So they set off towards home, the thought of seeing their family and friends again spurring them on.

However, in the next valley, things were happening that would have upset the gnomes had they known about them. The two elves who had been spying on the gnomes had reached Elfland and were telling the Duke and Duchess of Pointstick everything they knew about their planned expedition to rescue Potstop. The elves had been following the gnomes for a long time before they were discovered, and they had learned all about the magic potion and the effect it had on Tippit.

The Duke and Duchess looked concerned, Snitchmire and Prodlife skulked around looking their usual scheming, sneaky selves.

"We can't have gnomes going around rescuing solid ones," said the Duke.

"The humans will think we're stealing them back again."

"No one would trust us and the whole enterprise would fall apart and I wouldn't get any more of my beloved sparklies," spat the Duchess, fingering one of the massive diamond necklaces with the bony fingers of her left hand. Jewellery had become the elves' favourite item to trade for the gnomes and all of the jewellery had to be inspected by the Duchess. She always kept the largest and brightest items for herself, and the rest were distributed among the lady elves who were closest to the Duchess. This made her feel popular and loved.

They also traded the gnomes for cheeses and ham but the Duke's favourite was the fiery liquid that humans drank, which was far stronger than anything that they could steal from the gnomes.

So you can see that any disruption of their trade would be treated very seriously indeed by the elves, and the thought that trade might be stopped altogether was quite catastrophic.

So the elves started making plans to stop the gnomes. Elves can be very well organised at such times as these, and the Duke and

Duchess had rounded up all the most cunning elves, so they could discuss what to do.

"I think we should solidify all the gnomes," said one particularly belligerent character.

"Where would the future be if we did that? They wouldn't be able to produce anymore gnomes," said one of the deeper thinkers.

"Exactly what I was thinking," said the Duke.

"Can't we just solidify some of the gnomes?" Said Snitchmire.

"Yeah, go on, just a few," begged Prodlife.

"It's all right talking like this, but if the gnomes have enough of the magic potion we won't be able to solidify anyone," sneered the Duchess.

"Don't worry your pretty ugly head little about that, you stupid woman," said the Duke. "Do you really believe such a potion actually exists?"

"Well, the spies saw it working with their own eyes," answered the Duchess.

"They are probably blind as well as stupid," growled the Duke.

"But they are our best spies, you great stupid oaf," said the Duchess.

And so this banter went on and on. The Duke and Duchess always spoke to each other in an abusive manner in front of the other elves because they didn't want them to see that they actually liked each other. Liking each other would be seen as a weakness, and other elves, who might want to challenge the leadership of the Duke and Duchess, would be quick to spot such a weakness and use it to their advantage.

The banter continued until finally the Duke came up with a course of action.

"Right!" He said. "The first thing we must do is to sort out a band of elves to guard the entrance to the tunnel. If we stop the gnomes going in, there's no way they can rescue anybody."

"We can organise that," said Snitchmire and Prodlife together. "We'll take a group of the best fighting elves with us and camp round the entrance of the tunnel. The gnomes will be too scared to go anywhere near." They both sniggered at the thought of the gnomes trying to get to the tunnel.

"That's decided then," said the Duchess. "You horrible, slimy little toe rags. Go and round up your nastiest elves and get over to the tunnel as soon as possible."

Snitchmire and Prodlife were both cackling. There was nothing they enjoyed more than being insulted by the Duchess, and still cackling, they went off to gather their elfin gang.

Meanwhile Romanamor and Tippit had reached Tromort and Agninga's house. Tromort and Agninga were overjoyed to see the two adventurers and welcomed them warmly.

"It's fantastic to see you, we had our doubts whether you would make it back again," enthused Tromort.

Agninga lifted Tippit up and gave him a big kiss on the cheek. Tippit got very embarrassed by this and went a very bright shade of red.

"So did you find this Frogorf fellow?" Asked Tromort.

"Oh yes," said Romanamor. "In fact, he was far easier to find than we had dared hope." Romanamor went on to explain about the rows of stone statues leading to Frogorf's cave.

"And the potion?" Asked Tromort.

Romanamor explained all about the potion and how it had worked on Tippit.

"That is excellent news," said Tromort.

"We have left four flagons at the edge of the Grey Wood. Frogorf carried them for us, but he wouldn't venture any further into Gnomeland."

"At least there is hope now and I'd like to come with you if that's all right?" Said Tromort.

"Of course you can," said Romanamor. "There is a problem, however. The elves already know everything that we have planned."

"How come?" Asked Agninga anxiously.

Romanamor explained about the elves that had been spying on them, and how Frogorf had frightened them off.

"Shame he's not coming with us," said Tromort.

Romanamor and Tippit both agreed with that.

"I would feel much safer with him around," said Tippit. "He was built like four gnomes rolled into one."

"I'm afraid we're going to have to use more brainpower than muscle power if we are going to stay one step ahead of the elves," said Romanamor.

They all knew what he meant because they all knew how cunning and devious the elves could be.

"Would you like to rest for a while before you continue your journey?" Asked Agninga.

Romanamor and Tippit declined the offer, even though their legs were tired, the excitement of getting back home meant that they wanted to get moving as soon as possible.

Romanamor had an idea.

"Why doesn't Agninga come with us? I'm sure she'd be far happier in Grassroot in the company of other gnomes rather than waiting here all on her own."

"Yes, with the elves looking for trouble she'd be far safer in the village," agreed Tromort.

"Who will look after our crops?" Asked Agninga.

"Your safety comes first my dear, and I'm sure the crops can look after themselves for a few weeks," said Tromort.

"If you are gone for too long, we can send up a few gnomes from the village to keep an eye on things," said Romanamor. "We need to send some gnomes up here anyway to pick up the other flagons of potion."

After much thought Agninga finally agreed to go with them.

Tippit was getting impatient to be off, he'd never been away from home before and was missing his mum and Pullup, and although Great Uncle Gnong was usually grumpy towards the children, he was really missing him as well.

Finally everything was ready and they set off in convoy back towards Grassroot.

"Should be there in a few hours," said Romanamor happily.

The route back to Grassroot was mainly downhill and the gnomes made reasonable progress. Tippit by now was leading the convoy because the more excited he was getting, the faster he went. They didn't even stop for an afternoon break but continued on back towards home.

On the way they passed a few isolated cottages and were greeted with welcoming shouts from the gnomes who lived in them. Now, Romanamor was moving quicker and was keeping up with Tippit; Tromort and Agninga followed at their own leisurely pace. Soon they reached the outskirts of the village. News of their arrival travelled very quickly through the village and by the time they were halfway through, Cramarc, Pullup and

Gnong had heard of their return. By the time their cottage came into view, Cramarc and Pullup were running up the main street towards them, Gnong followed as fast as his old legs would carry him.

A very emotional moment followed, and considering that gnomes very seldom have these moments, this was an emotional deluge. Romanamor and Tippit stopped when they saw Cramarc and Pullup running towards them. They put down their baggage and the flagons they were carrying and just stood there with tears in their eyes, big wide smiles on their faces and arms outstretched waiting to hug their loved ones. Cramarc rushed into Romanamor's arms with such force that she sent him flying backwards. They lay hugging each other for a while, then they got slowly to their feet looking rather embarrassed. Tippit and Pullup meanwhile, were dancing around holding each others arms doing some kind of excited jig, until they realised half the eyes in the village were watching them. Everyone that was not off working in the fields had come out to welcome them home.

Gnong arrived and went over to give Tippit a great big hug.

"Welcome home," he said. "We thought we might never see you again."

"And we thought we might never see you again," said Tippit tearfully.

"Nonsense, I had every faith that we could make it back here without too much trouble," said Romanamor, trying to put a brave face on things. But the underlying tremor in his voice gave away the fact that he too had his doubts whether they would return safely.

Tromort and Agninga had now caught up with the others, and they trudged up the main street, a little bit bemused by all the attention they were receiving.

"And who might they be?" Asked Gnong.

Romanamor introduced them to the family and explained that Tromort, whose son Naggan had been kidnapped, was coming with them to Humanland.

"That is good news indeed," said Gnong. "Another adult male gnome would come in very useful."

"Anyway that's enough chit-chat," said Cramarc. "I expect you are all tired and hungry after your journey. Come back to the cottage and I'll get you some supper."

"Sounds good to me," said Tromort. "I'm starving."

"So what's in the flagons?" Asked Gnong.

"More good news, Uncle. We have managed to acquire some of the bravery potion and it actually works," said Romanamor.

He went on to explain how the potion had been used to revive Tippit.

"So Frogorf is still alive, eh?" Asked Gnong.

"Yes, he's alive, and he's stronger and fitter than any other gnome in Gnomeland," answered Tippit.

Romanamor went on to explain about the stone statues and about everything else that had happened on their journey.

"I'm just glad you've returned home safely," said Cramarc. "Now come along and have something to eat and we can discuss what we are going to do next."

So they walked slowly down the main street back to their cottage. Romanamor and Cramarc walked arm in arm. Tippit and Pullup were walking alongside with Tippit talking non-stop about his big adventure. Gnong, Tromort and Agninga brought up the rear. Gnong had heard of Tromort and Agninga, and was asking them all sorts of questions about how they managed to survive in such an isolated place.

"I suppose we've grown used to it over the years," said Tromort. "But now, without Naggan, life has become very dull, he was a good gnome and we miss him very much."

"I'm sure you do," sympathised Gnong. "Still, now you have the potion, at least there's some hope of getting him back."

They arrived at the cottage where they were welcomed by their nearest neighbours, who had actually put up a banner pronouncing, *Welcome Home* across the top of the doorway. A delicious aroma wafted through the air.

"Mmm, cauliflower and parsnip stew if I'm not mistaken," said Romanamor.

He was right. Two of the female gnomes who lived down the road had taken the liberty of using Cramarc's stove to make a huge cauldron of their favourite stew. Within a few minutes, they were sat down at the table spooning the stew into their mouths as fast as they could. The familiar loud slurping noises that gnomes make when they're hungry were the only sounds to be heard for a while.

"Wonderful food!" Said Tromort, breaking the silence. "I haven't tasted such delicious stew for a long time."

Agninga, quite rightly, looked hurt by this comment.

"Sorry dear, there's nothing wrong with your cooking, it's just that we don't have the right ingredients up where we live," apologised Tromort.

"Anybody for anymore?" Asked Cramarc.

They were so hungry that they eagerly accepted the offer of a second helping. These bowls of stew disappeared almost as quickly as the first ones. After they had finished eating, the gnomes relaxed for a while with cool drinks of water brought down from the nearby stream.

"You look absolutely worn out," said Cramarc to the four gnomes sat round the table.

"I think you all need a good night's rest."

"Tromort and Agninga can use my bed out in the annex; I can use Potstop's bed for the time being," said Gnong.

"That's very kind of you," said Agninga. "I'm so tired I could sleep for a week."

Tippit had already fallen asleep at the table, his head bent forward, resting on his arms.

"I'll carry Tippit to his bed and then I'm going to bed myself," yawned Romanamor.

So the four exhausted gnomes went off to bed whilst Cramarc and the two friendly neighbours cleared away the dinner things.

Despite their exhaustion, everyone awoke early the next morning, eager to start making plans for their journey into Humanland. Everyone that is, except Tippit, who carried on sleeping through most of the day.

"Morning everyone," said Cramarc, who was already up cooking breakfast.

They sat round the large table whilst Cramarc dished up the traditional gnomish breakfast, consisting of fried vegetables and crusty bread washed down with nettle tea.

When the munching and slurping had finished, they sat in silence for a while, pondering on how best to start the discussion about the families' expedition. One by one the gnomes turned to look in the direction of Gnong, who, as the oldest and therefore wisest, was expected to start the discussion.

Gnong sat deep in thought for a while, trying to put the ideas in his head into a logical order, finally he spoke.

"The first thing we must do is arrange for some gnomes to go up to the Grey Wood to collect the rest of the potion."

"I agree," said Romanamor. "But they will have to be very careful because the elves will be watching every move we make."

"That's true," said Gnong. "I'll speak with the elders and see if we can arrange for some of the builders from Stonemarble to go up there, as they are by far the strongest gnomes and the elves would think twice before taking them on."

"Maybe we could use some of the builders to guard the entrance to the cave when we go through to Humanland," said Cramarc.

"Good idea," answered Gnong. "We'll have to organise it through the elders as we can't do anything without their agreement."

"So we must arrange this meeting as soon as we can," said Romanamor. "But this time we must all attend because we are the ones who are going to be risking our lives by going to Humanland."

"I don't know if that will be allowed," said Gnong.

"No one but the elders have ever attended the meetings."

"I'm sure they will make an exception in our case," said Cramarc confidently.

"Very well," said Gnong. "I'll have a word with Corabaroc."

"Good, that's settled then," said Romanamor. "Now we must decide who is going on this expedition and who is staying behind."

"Maybe we should all go," said Cramarc.

"Except me of course," said Gnong. "I'm too old to walk any distance nowadays."

"I'd like to go." Agninga said. "I don't think I could bear waiting here wondering if Tromort would ever come home."

"That's all right my dear," comforted Tromort. "I'd rather have you with me even though you would be much safer here."

As they had been together for so many years, it would not be fair to leave Agninga behind, and it was agreed by everyone that she should go.

The next thing they needed to consider was what supplies they needed to take with them. Romanamor, who had a very logical mind, drew up a list of the minimum amount of food and drink that they would need to take with them.

He worked out the daily ration for two children and four adults. Then estimated the number of days they were going to be away. When Romanamor had reached a total, his heart sank.

"We'll never be able to carry this amount of supplies. Plus the potion that we're going to need," he said despondently.

"Work it out again, maybe we can survive on less," said Cramarc.

"I've worked it out to the bare minimum as it is. We'll have to find some other way of carrying it all."

"Maybe there is a way," said Gnong, who had been thinking deeply about the problem. "Maybe the gnome who makes the carts that the builders use to carry their stone could make a smaller one that ordinary sized gnomes could pull."

"Brilliant idea," said Tromort. "I'd like to volunteer to go to Stonemarble and ask him. I've met him in the past and he seems to be quite a friendly little gnome and I'm sure he's quite capable of making us a cart."

"That's settled then," said Gnong. "The sooner we can get things moving the better. I'll go and see Corabaroc and arrange a meeting with the elders for this evening."

Gnong set off to arrange the meeting, Tromort went off to see the cart maker and the rest busied themselves in the gardens selecting the fruit and vegetables for the journey. Even Tippit and Pullup helped with just the picking. They were as anxious to be off as everyone else was.

Tromort arrived at the cart makers by late afternoon. The cart maker, whose name was Cattac, said that he would be glad to help, and with the aid of his apprentices he could produce a smaller version of a builder's cart in a couple of days.

Tromort sat watching the cart-making gnomes as they set to work. Cattac was probably one of the happiest gnomes Tromort had ever met. He whistled most of the time when he was working and when he wasn't whistling, he would break into song. Occasionally, one of the builder gnomes would turn up with a cart to be repaired, or, if it was beyond repair, to order a new one. Tromort chatted to the builders, enjoying this newly found social outlet after living in isolation for so long.

The builders had heard of the plans the family were making to rescue their son and they asked Tromort if there was any way that they could help. Tromort explained about the possible need for someone to guard the tunnel entrance to stop the elves from getting in.

He wasn't sure whether to mention the need to collect the four flagons of magic potion without first asking the council of elders. He thought about it for a while and came to the conclusion that he should say something because they needed to retrieve the flagons as soon as possible.

The builders that he mentioned it to said that they would gladly pick up the potion and if they timed it right, they would be back before Cattac and his apprentices had finished making the cart. Tromort explained the exact location of the flagons to the builders and they set off immediately in the direction of the Grey Wood.

Tromort chatted to Cattac about the need to guard the tunnel entrance.

"It's all a question," he said to Cattac. "Of how many builders you can spare."

Cattac reckoned that the building trade in Stonemarble was fairly quiet at the moment and therefore quite a few of the builders could be recruited as guards.

"That is good news," said Tromort, beginning to see things in a more optimistic light than he had before.

Back in Grassroot, things were beginning to happen with equal speed. All the supplies had been collected and were safely tucked away in the food store. The meeting with the elders was imminent, and the family was walking together towards the communal hut in the centre of the village. When they arrived, they were welcomed at the door by Corabaroc himself.

"Come in, come in," he said. "Welcome to the council. If I sound a little impatient it's because we need to get everything moving as soon as possible. There has been a lot of elfin activity in the region and they seem to know that something is going on."

The council of elders was already sat around the table. Some spare chairs had been placed at the far end, so that Romanamor and company could take an active part in the meeting. Corabaroc sat in his chair at the head of the table. There was an urgency in his voice that had seldom been heard before.

"First of all," he said, "I'd like to welcome the brave family to our meeting. Now as you all know they are off to Humanland to rescue, not only their child, but maybe some of the other children as well. We need to get them under way as soon as possible, because a large number of elves have been seen, particularly around the entrance to the caves," he paused for breath then continued. "There is some very good news from Stonemarble. Your friend Tromort has organised some builders to go and collect the rest of the potion and also the construction of the cart is well under way." He paused for another breath, longer this time, as he was collecting his thoughts for the final part of the speech. Everyone sat around the table patiently, they all understood that gnomes are not used to making long speeches.

"Now this journey of yours is probably the single most important event to happen in Gnomeland for many years and the elders of Grassroot and of Stonemarble have decided to give you our fullest backing, in other words we will assist you in any way we can."

"Hear! Hear!" Said Wollow. "It's time we stood up to these elves and showed them that they can't get away with kidnapping our children."

"True," said Barrab. "But we must not forget how nasty and devious the elves can be."

"Yes," said Corabaroc. "Let's not get carried away with thoughts of war. Us gnomes have been peace-loving for so long, we need to treat every situation with extreme caution."

"Nevertheless I'd still like to see the elves taught a lesson!" Said Wollow forcefully.

"Wouldn't we all?" Answered Corabaroc. "Wouldn't we all?"

"So how long are the builders expected to keep the elves away from the tunnel entrance?" Asked Garfrag.

"I think a couple of days should be long enough. A day and a half for the family to get through the tunnel, and then half a day for them to get clear on the other side," said Martram, who had been studying past records to find out things, such as the length of the tunnel.

"And how long do you intend staying in Humanland?" Asked Garfrag, looking towards Romanamor.

"I'm not too sure. I think we can carry enough supplies for about three days," answered Romanamor. "But there's no way of telling if it will be long enough."

"Well if everything goes according to plan and you manage to get back unharmed, we can always organise another expedition for later on," said Corabaroc.

"Yes, we can," said Barrab. "The main thing is that you all get back here safely."

"The other thing I've worked out is how many torches you will need to light your way in the tunnel," said Martram.

Ah yes, torches. I'd forgotten all about them," said Romanamor. "So how many will we need?"

"Well," answered Martram. "If we work on the basis that each torch lasts for three hours, and you will be in the tunnel for approximately three days, you will need 24 torches. Twelve on the way there and 12 on the way back."

"Thanks Martram," said Romanamor.

"Hopefully we can hide the torches we need for the return journey somewhere near the other end of the tunnel."

"Well that seems to be everything taken care of," said Corabaroc.

"Now if there is anything else you need just let us know. For now, I suggest you get plenty of rest before Tromort returns, because you will need all your energy for the expedition."

Meanwhile Sullus, who until now had been silent, was pouring a small measure of carrot whiskey into some mugs and passing them round to everyone, except Pullup and Tippit, who were far too young to drink anything alcoholic. Instead he gave them some strawberry juice, an acknowledged favourite drink among young gnomes. When finally everyone had a drink in front of them, Sullus raised his mug and invited the others to do the same.

"Here's to a safe return of our intrepid adventurers," he said, as loudly as he could, which wasn't very loud at all, but could just be heard at the other end of the table.

"And here's to the success of the potion, and to Frogorf who made such a potion possible," said Sullus getting a bit carried away with his duties as toastmaster.

"Thank you Sullus," said Corabaroc. "I too would like to wish them a safe journey and that just about brings the meeting to a close. Thank you all for coming."

It may seem like a very sudden end to the meeting but Corabaroc's great age was showing and he wanted to go home to bed.

They all slept soundly that night as they had all been thinking very hard during the meeting, something that does not come naturally to gnomes, and had needed a lot of effort.

The next day passed uneventfully with the family just lazing around and taking things easy. The neighbours were coming in doing the cooking and cleaning so that all the family could get maximum amount of rest.

It was mid-afternoon on the following day that things started to liven up. News of Tromort's return reached the ears of Gnong, who was working in the vegetable patch. He hurried home as fast as his old legs would carry him.

"Tromort's back," he announced as he walked through the doorway.

"He's walking through the village this very minute."

Agninga shot straight of her chair, raced out the hut and ran up the main street of the village towards Tromort. He was walking quite slowly as he had been pushing the cart for a long time and was exhausted but when he saw Agninga he sped up slightly and a huge grin spread across his face. He stopped pushing the cart and gave Agninga a long hug. Even though Tromort had only been away for a couple of days, it was the first time that they had been apart for quite a few years and they were really pleased to be back together again.

Strapped safely to the cart were the four flagons of magic potion that had been hidden in the Grey Wood, and once the supplies of food and drink were loaded on to it, the gnomes would be able to start their journey.

"Tromort needs a rest first," said Agninga looking into her husband's weary eyes.

"Of course he does," replied Romanamor. "If he gets a good night's sleep, hopefully we can all be ready to move off at sunrise."

So Tromort went off for a well-earned rest, while the other gnomes busied themselves loading up the cart. Cramarc was organising the loading because with gnomes, as with humans, the females are far better at packing things for journeys and making use of all available space. She loaded the cart in the order that things would be needed, adding an extra flagon of potion to the load. The extra flagon was for the builders who were going to defend this end of the tunnel, because even though the builders were quite large and strong, they still had the non-aggressive minds of ordinary gnomes and underneath their brash exterior were quite timid. At last the cart was fully loaded.

Everything on it was secured, as they didn't want things falling off en route. Some of the neighbours agreed to stay up all night and guard it just in case there was elves about.

So Romanamor, Cramarc, Tippit, Pullup and Agninga went off to bed. Sleep was very restless for all of them as they were filled with a mixture of excitement and fear about their forthcoming adventure. Tromort however slept soundly on, the sound of his loud snoring echoing around the walls of the cottage. Tromort had done well and his effort was appreciated by the others. But the journey back hadn't been quite as easy as he had made out. Whilst he was walking, he felt eyes watching him from every direction and once or twice he had seen an elf dart behind a tree or a rock. For some reason known only to them, the elves didn't attack Tromort, but kept a respectable distance from him. Nevertheless Tromort was in constant fear that they might attack and it was this fear that kept him moving. In fact he kept moving without a break all the way back to Grassroot. On his return he decided not to mention the elf spies to the others, as he did not want to worry them unnecessarily. Things would, he had no doubt, become scary enough in the weeks to come.

Chapter 4

The Start of the Great Adventure

The night passed without incident and the gnomes were getting out of bed just as the sun began peering over the mountain tops in the distance. The sky was clear blue with just a few puffy white clouds floating gently across it.

"Lovely day for an adventure," said Romanamor to nobody in particular.

The neighbours were busy in the kitchen making a light breakfast for everyone. Nobody was particularly hungry, I guess that the term butterflies in the stomach, would apply to how the gnomes were feeling that morning.

"You must eat something," Cramarc was insisting. "We have a long day ahead and we need food to give us energy."

So everyone ate what little food they could manage, except for Tromort that is, whose appetite was huge owing to the fact that he hadn't eaten for two days.

"It's nice to have a home cooked meal again," he said contentedly.

Romanamor was making sure that the straps holding the supplies onto the cart were secure. Finally he was satisfied.

"That's it. Is everyone ready to go?"

"I think so," said Cramarc, having a final look round her beloved home.

"Where's Gnong this morning?"

"He went off early to have a word with Corabaroc, making sure that everything was organised with the builders," answered Romanamor.

"We'd better hang on until he gets back," said Cramarc. "I'm sure he'll want to see us before we go."

"Here he is now," said Tromort, and sure enough, there he was, slowly walking up the track, the other elders alongside and everyone else in the village following closely behind.

So the family said their tearful farewells to their friends and neighbours and slowly set off up the track towards the mountains, which were located on the other side of the lake.

Romanamor was pushing the cart, Cramarc was walking beside him. Tromort and Agninga were following closely behind, whilst

Tippit and Pullup were racing on ahead. They were racing a bit too far ahead for Cramarc's liking.

"Slow down a bit you two," she said. "We need to take things slowly so that we can conserve our energy for later on."

"Sorry Mum," they said in unison, and both slowed down to the same pace as everyone else. Gnome children were on the whole well-behaved and usually obeyed what their parents said, without question. The little group was soon walking along the shore of the lake and Grassroot was becoming more distant. Eventually all they could see of their home village were the plumes of smoke rising from the chimneys.

"This is it then," said Romanamor. "No turning back now, we've made our choice."

"Let's just hope it's the right one," said Cramarc with a hint of speculation in her voice.

The gnomes continued around the lake at their slow, almost reluctant pace. The entrance to the tunnel was about a day's journey away and it was soon time to leave the comforting shores of the lake and head out across open country towards the mountains.

As you already know, gnomes have an uncanny sense of direction and seem to be able to get to where they want to go without the aid of maps or compasses, which was just as well because maps and compasses were unknown in Gnomeland. As there was no actual track, it was hard work pushing the cart through the long grass and it took two gnomes to actually keep it moving.

"This isn't as easy as I thought," puffed Romanamor.

Cramarc and Agninga took turns helping to push. Progress was slow but they were still moving and they were still headed in the right direction.

"Ho on, kool!" Exclaimed Agninga, suddenly pointing ahead. "A revir!"

"Ho ym," said Cramarc, also slipping back into backwards speech.

"Woh era ew gniog ot teg ssorca?"

As they approached the river, they could see that it was slow moving and fairly wide. Tromort and Romanamor were still struggling with the cart and were too breathless to speak, whereas Tippit and Pullup had run on ahead to the river. Before anyone could shout a warning, they had run straight in and were leaping around and splashing each other, happy at the release from just plodding along beside the cart.

"It looks quite shallow," said Agninga, regaining her composure.

"Thank goodness for that," agreed Cramarc.

"We'll still never get the cart across, it's too heavy," said Romanamor.

"We'll have to unload it first and then carry everything across separately."

"More time wasted," grumbled Tromort. "If things get any slower, we'll never reach the safety of the builder's camp by nightfall."

"Cheer up my friend," said Romanamor. "We can have a rest once we've crossed the river and maybe, with renewed energy, we can still make it."

So with the incentive of having a rest and something to eat, they set to work unloading the cart. The children began ferrying things across to the other side. In fact they managed to carry everything over except for the potion. The adults decided it was a too valuable a commodity to risk being spilled in the river, and carried the potion themselves.

At last all the supplies were safely across and with a lot of heaving and pushing, they got the cart across as well. They re-loaded the cart, leaving off a few items of food, which they had picked out for their lunch. They had just settled down to eat when Tromort raised his large head upwards, sniffing the air as he did so.

"Elves," he whispered. "I can smell them a mile off."

All the Gnomes began furtively sniffing the air and they all recognised the rancid, unwashed stench of elves.

"If we're going to have a rest, we'd better have some of the potion first," said Romanamor.

"Good idea," said Cramarc.

They managed to pour a small amount of the potion into a mug, then they passed it round and took a few sips each.

"How long will the effect last?" Wondered Agninga out loud.

"Nobody knows," said Romanamor. We'll just have to use our discretion. I'm sure we'll know when the effect is wearing off."

The potion left in the mug was carefully poured back into the flagon and the gnomes settled down for a well-deserved rest. Pullup and Tippit agreed to stay alert as they had more energy than the adults and didn't need the rest quite so much. Whilst the adults rested, Pullup and Tippit became aware of a rustling sound in a nearby clump of bushes. The scent of the elves suddenly become stronger and from the bushes emerged two wickedly grinning elves.

"What have we here then?" Said one of the elves.

"Looks like a couple of unguarded young gnomes," answered the other one.

"Shall we take them away with us?" Said the first elf, sneering.

"Nice easy profit for us if we do," said the other one.

"If we move quickly, they won't have time to wake the adults."

So the elves moved menacingly towards Pullup and Tippit. The gnomes, as you can imagine, were terrified. Two questions went through their minds, do they wake the adults, who obviously needed their rest, or do they trust that the potion works and they do not solidify? The questions answered themselves, for as they stood there, they felt a strength rising within, not an aggressive strength, but a kind of calm inner strength, whereby they knew that the elves could not harm them, well not to the point of solidity anyway. The elves were confused, they had threatened young gnomes before and usually they had gone solid without too much trouble but these gnomes were somehow different.

The elves started making nasty threats.

"Maybe we could take one away and make a nice stew with it," suggested one.

"Mmm, nothing I like better than a hot gnome stew," retorted the other.

"You don't scare us," said Tippit, shakily.

"Sey ew era regnorts won," said Pullup, unable to keep his speech forwards.

"What did you say?" Asked the first elf.

"He said, we are stronger now, and there's no way we are going to go solid," announced Tippit.

"Right, we'll have to carry you off as you are then," said the second elf. "Maybe you'll go solid later."

"Just try it," threatened Pullup.

The elves pounced on Pullup, their foetid breath hot in his face and with their sharp fingernails digging into his skin, they started dragging him off.

Just then Romanamor woke up. Realising what was happening he got up on his feet as quickly as he could, grabbed a nearby rock and ran straight at the elves, holding the rock over his head. Now a gnome with a contorted look of anger on his face, was a new sight to an elf and they let go of Pullup straight away. Romanamor kept up his charge and the elves turned tail and ran as fast as their spindly legs could carry them.

"We'll be right back," said the first elf over his shoulder. "You haven't seen the last of us."

"And there won't just be two of us next time," said the other one.

"Are you all right?" Asked Romanamor as he reached his sons.

"I kniht os," said Pullup, shakily.

"Just a few scratches, I think," said Tippit.

"Thanks Dad," said Pullup. "That potion really works, I've never seen you so aggressive before."

"I think desperate would be a better word. I don't want another son of mine to get taken by the elves."

By now the other gnomes were waking up.

"What's been going on?" Asked Cramarc sleepily.

Romanamor explained what had happened and went on to say that the elves would certainly be back and there was no time to lose.

"We must get moving straight away," he said. "If we hurry, we may just beat the elves to the builder's camp."

The gnomes set off with renewed energy. In fact, they moved faster than they had before, as the effect of the potion had not yet worn off. The fact that they were going uphill all of the time, did not seem to adversely affect their progress. The thought of the elves returning made them more determined than ever. Pullup and Tippit were walking slightly ahead of the rest, keeping an eye out for any sign of elves.

They travelled on for a few more miles, their progress made a bit easier by the fact that the long grass had given way to much shorter grass interspersed by the occasional clump of purple mountain heather.

They were climbing more steeply now as they neared the mountains and two gnomes were required to push the cart at all times. Cramarc or Agninga took over from one of male gnomes occasionally to give them a break.

A distant noise was beginning to worry the family. They could hear the sound of rushing water a long time before they could see the next hazard blocking their way.

"Another river," said Cramarc despondently. "And this one looks wider than the last one."

"And deeper too," said Romanamor. "Maybe if we walk upstream, it will become easier to cross."

So they turned and walked upstream but the flow of water didn't to ease up at all. They were just about to despair when they saw an amazing geographical occurrence. A huge pile of rocks had fallen from the mountains above and formed a natural bridge over the river. Over the years, the river had worn a channel beneath the rocks, leaving the top fairly dry. Although it looked uneven, the gnomes thought it would be possible to walk across.

"The trouble is, how are we going to get the cart to the other side?" Asked Tromort. "We can't wheel it over because it's far too rocky."

"Well we certainly can't leave it here; I don't know what we're going to do."

Just then a deep voice boomed across the river.

"Hello! Are you stuck? Do you need any help?" It was one of the builders, who had been patrolling the far side of the river.

"Yes, we do please, we can't get our cart across the bridge!" Romanamor shouted back.

"Hold on while I go and get some more builders." Came the answering boom. "I presume that you're the lot we're all here to protect."

"That's right we are." Answered Romanamor.

"You've no need to worry then, we'll get you across in no time," and with that the builder marched off to get help.

"We may as well take it easy for a while until he gets back and this time we'll all be looking out for elves," said Romanamor.

The little band of adventurers took full advantage of the spare time. Cramarc unpacked a few of the rations whilst Tromort collected some fresh water from the river. The gnomes kept a vigilant lookout whilst they munched their food and took long refreshing swigs of the cool water.

Soon the builder returned accompanied by three of his friends. They walked across the rock bridge and came over to where the family was sitting.

"We've had plenty of practise at crossing the rocks," said the builder.

"You may not find it quite so easy, so we've brought some rope. If we tie you all together and one of you falls, we will be able to save them."

"That's very thoughtful of you," said Agninga, who was looking extremely nervous at the thought of going over.

"We're only here to help," said the builder. "By the way, my name's Granarg and these are my work mates Roccor, Toocoot and Taffat."

"Very pleased to meet you," Romanamor said, introducing his own family and friends to the builders.

Dusk was beginning to fall, and because Gnomeland was surrounded by mountains, dusk very quickly turns into night.

"Right, we've no time to lose," said Granarg, looping and tying the rope around Romanamor and then looping the rope around the others and tying it around Tromort at the end of the line. Granarg had deliberately used the strongest gnomes as anchor men because if anyone slipped, there was a better chance of stopping them from falling into the river.

"It's too tight," moaned Pullup.

"You won't be thinking that it's too tight if it saves your life," said his mum crossly. "Now stop grumbling and let's get moving."

So the gnomes, led by Romanamor, tentatively stepped onto the bridge. To any bystander, they would have looked a strange sight, all tied together, slowly shuffling their way across the rocks. It was with great relief that they reached the other side without mishap.

"Well done!" Shouted Granarg from the other side. "We'll be over right away!"

And with that, the four builder gnomes picked up a corner each of the cart and carried it across the bridge.

"You made that look easy," said Tromort.

"Practise, Tromort, practise. We've been here for a while and have crossed the bridge many times with our own supplies," answered Granarg.

"Just a short walk to the camp from here," said Roccor. "I expect you're hungry, we've always got a pot of cauliflower and parsnip stew on the boil."

"Sounds tempting," said Tromort. "We've been eating raw food all day."

The builders pushed the cart up to the camp. When they arrived there, the gnomes were surprised at how well the builders were organised. They had built temporary shelters with loose stones and somehow managed to put roofs on them by arranging the stones in such a way that they met in the middle across the top.

"Very clever," said Romanamor. "How did you manage to build them so quickly?"

"Our trade," answered Granarg. "We've been building for so many years that it comes naturally to us wherever we are."

"I'm afraid we haven't got much in the way of furniture," said Roccor, gesturing the gnomes into one of the huts. We've managed to make a couple of benches, so at least you can sit down while you eat."

Builders didn't have much time for luxuries, as they spent most of the daylight hours working. Another builder emerged through the doorway of the makeshift kitchen.

"Right, who's hungry?" He asked.

They all readily admitted that they were starving.

"Sit yourselves down and I'll be right back with your food," he said.

Moments later he was back carrying two huge steaming bowls of cauliflower and parsnip stew. Two other builders came into the room also carrying bowls of stew. Builders have massive appetites and they had forgotten that ordinary gnomes would never eat a builder's sized meal.

"Don't worry if you can't eat it all," said Roccor, realising the family's dilemma. "We can tip what's left back into the pot, so it won't be wasted."

Thank goodness for that, I wouldn't have been able to eat a whole bowl-full, thought Agninga to herself.

The gnomes sat silently eating as much of the stew as they could, although Tromort was the only one to come anywhere near emptying his bowl.

"Wonderful stew," remarked Romanamor, thanking the builder chefs. "I couldn't eat another drop."

The builders cleared away the bowls from the table.

"Right, we had better make some plans to get you lot safely through the tunnel," suggested Granarg. "The elves are camped very near to the tunnel entrance and the first thing to do is to get them out of the way."

"How many are there?" Asked Romanamor.

"At the last count between 20 and 25, but they are steadily increasing their numbers all the time," answered Granarg.

"Do you think you can keep them out of the way long enough?"

"Maybe, maybe not. It depends on how many more are on their way."

"We've bought an extra flagon of Frogorf's potion with us, if it will help."

"It may do, we'll try anything once."

"I think we had better rest for a while before we do anything," said Romanamor.

"Pullup and Tippit look absolutely worn out."

"We've got a few straw mattresses you can use," said Roccor. "They may not be luxury but they're more comfortable than sleeping on the bare floor."

The family, grateful for the hospitality the builders had shown them, settled down for the night.

The builders carried on talking, making plans for getting the elves away from the tunnel entrance.

"I think we ought to attack the elves' camp just before dawn, as most of them will be sleeping," said the curiously named Toocoot.

"Good thinking," agreed Granarg. "We need the element of surprise on our side if we are to scare them away."

The builders talked into the night. After building the huts, they spent most of their days at the camp just lazing around, this was something that they weren't used to. As they weren't using much energy, they were able to stay awake and continue talking until their plans were complete, after which they did decide to rest for a while. One of the builders stayed up to guard the camp and make sure everyone woke up a couple of hours before dawn.

The night passed without incident. The elves kept a respectable distance from the builder's camp, but you can be sure that their spies were out there somewhere.

The builder guarding the camp made use of the time by checking the cart and making sure everything was tied on securely. He walked round the outskirts of the camp, nose tilted upwards checking for the rancid smell of the elves, but all seemed clear. When the time came, he went round waking everybody up. One by one the sleepy gnomes rose from their beds. Granarg briefly outlined the plan to Romanamor and the others. Romanamor said it was a good plan and they would be ready to go, straight away.

"Time we made a move then," said Granarg. "We must be at the elves' camp before daybreak."

Romanamor went to the cart and came back with a flagon of the potion.

"We had better all have some of this before we go," he said, pouring the precious liquid carefully into some mugs and passing them around.

"Mmm, doesn't taste too bad at all, in fact I could get used to drinking this," said Roccor, having another swig.

"Careful not to drink too much," exclaimed Granarg. "Don't forget we have to make it last for quite a while."

"I'll put it back on the cart," hastened Tromort. "You may need it at the tunnel."

"Everybody ready to move?" Asked Granarg.

"Yes, all ready," answered Romanamor.

"Good, let's go then," enthused Granarg, already feeling the effects of the potion.

"Let's go and sort out these nasty little vermin."

The builders marched in army style, two abreast with the family bringing up the rear. A couple of the builders held back to help push the cart. The going was fairly easy as the path had been trodden many times before and the family, with the help of the builders, found it quite easy to keep up.

"We should be close to the elves' camp within half an hour," said Granarg. "Have you got your torches ready for when you enter the tunnel?"

"We've packed them on top of the cart, so we can get them easily," answered Tromort.

For the rest of the way, the entourage travelled in silence. The family were far too busy thinking about what they were going to do to talk much, and the builder gnomes, for the most part, did not talk anyway.

They were nearing the elves' camp now and they could just make out the tunnel entrance through the gloom.

"You'd better wait here," whispered Granarg. "While we go to the camp and give the elves the biggest shock of their lives."

"Good luck," wished Romanamor.

"Luck! We don't need luck!" Exclaimed Roccor. "We're going to scare the little blighters out of their wits."

"Oh dear, I think that extra swig of the potion's gone to his head," feared Granarg.

"Just remember, these are elves we're trying to scare and the only way we can do it is if we keep cool heads on our shoulders."

"Sorry," said Roccor. "I'll try not to get too carried away."

"You'll be carried away alright if you don't stay calm," said Toocoot under his breath.

"Come on then," whispered Granarg. "But remember to stay very quiet."

They approached the elves' camp very stealthily indeed. The camp itself wasn't organised like the builder's camp; the elves were just strewn about everywhere. There were some under blankets, but most of them were just lying in the open air, their long noses pointing towards the night sky. The remnants of a fire still had a few glowing embers and quite a few elves had fallen asleep near it to try and stay warm.

Granarg looked all around the camp, counting the elves as he did so. About 30 he thought to himself.

"Take half a dozen gnomes and place them around the perimeter of the camp," he whispered to Toocoot. "Get them all to pick up a large stone or stick because they need to look as menacing as possible. I'll raise my arms in the air as a signal to attack."

Toocoot did as he was asked and soon all the gnomes were in position. Granarg stood silently in the half-gloom his gaze sweeping over the elves' camp making sure everything was ready.

Completely satisfied he raised his arms stiffly into the air.

"Attack the elves!" He shouted at the top of his voice. The other builders followed his example, and soon they were all leaping about holding rocks or sticks above their heads shouting, "Attack the elves! Attack the elves!"

All the elves sat bolt upright at the same time. They looked more shocked than terrified as they watched the mad, dancing, chanting gnomes. To them this scene was unbelievable. Gnomes didn't attack elves. In their history it was always the elves that attacked the gnomes.

It wasn't until one or two of the builders began hitting them with sticks that they realised that these gnomes were serious.

One by one the elves were getting to their feet and trying to fight back. But there was no way they were going to overcome these mad gnomes, and eventually they all ran off shrieking into the nearby forest. It was getting lighter now and from where they were hidden, Romanamor and company could see everything that was going on.

"It's now or never," he said to the others. He motioned to them and they set off quietly in the direction of the tunnel entrance.

The commotion in the elves' camp continued until the builders were sure that the last of the elves had gone. Granarg walked quickly over to the tunnel so he could wish the family good luck.

"The elves will be back," he warned. "And next time we won't be able to take them by surprise. So make haste while you can, and we'll keep this end clear for as long as possible."

Chapter 5

Negotiating the Caves and on to Humanland

The family thanked Granarg for all he had done, then said their farewells and made their way into the tunnel.

They could see where they were going for the first few hundred metres but after that they had to light one of the torches. Pullup and Tippit were scared and stayed very close to their parents.

"So far, so good," said Tromort, his voice echoing around the walls of the cave.

They were too intent on reaching the other end to think about eating or sleeping. The thought that the elves might come spurred them on and they carried on walking at a fairly fast pace.

The first torch was coming to an end, so they lit the second one before it went out. They did the same with the third torch and so on, as they didn't want to be left in darkness at all. They had been walking for a long time when they came to a point where the tunnel split into two. "Which way do we go?" Asked Cramarc, anxiously.

"Well, according to the elders it doesn't matter because both tunnels end up where we want to go," answered Tromort.

"Let's take the left one then," said Romanamor, getting ready to light another torch.

"Agreed," said Tromort.

The strange convoy carried on and on, their poor little legs getting wearier by the minute.

"Is this tunnel never going to end?" Asked Tippit.

"My legs are aching and my feet are sore," moaned Pullup.

"We can't rest until we reach the other end," said Romanamor. "You don't want the elves to catch up with us do you?"

"No we don't," said Pullup and Tippit together.

"Have courage my children, I'm sure it won't be long before we're out of here," encouraged Cramarc.

The torches were being used up faster than the gnomes had anticipated. Romanamor had just lit up the fourteenth one and was wondering how far out Martram had been with his calculations, when they rounded a sharp bend and there, in the distance, was a little pinprick of light.

“At last,” said Agninga. “I thought we were stuck in here forever.”

“Only trouble is, we haven’t got enough torches left to see our way coming back,” said Tromort.

“I’m sure we’ll be all right, the elves come through all the time without using torches,” speculated Romanamor.

“Let’s worry about that if we get back here safely, shall we?” Said Cramarc. “We’ve got enough to worry about for the time being.” Everyone knew that Cramarc was right, the main thing was getting back safely.

The pinprick of light was growing gradually larger as they neared the exit. They could see where they were going now, without the use of torches. Pullup and Tippit were getting bolder and rushing on ahead of the rest.

“Don’t go too far ahead, there may be elves about,” warned Romanamor.

Pullup and Tippit calmed down at the very mention of the word elves and they ran back to be closer to the others for safety.

The little group approached the exit very cautiously, they noticed the large clumps of prickly bushes that the elves had planted to hide it.

“Wait here and be quiet,” said Romanamor. "I’m going to have a look round just to check there are no elves nearby.”

It took him a while to make sure there were no elves, and only when he was completely satisfied that this was the case, did he return to the others. He did find a pile of freshly chewed bones, indicating that they had been there recently, but there was no sign of the elves.

"All clear," he said when he got back. "But we must move quickly as there are signs that the elves have been here."

"Can we have some food first please? I'm starving," asked Tippit.

"All right then, I must admit I'm quite hungry myself," conceded Romanamor. "But we must be moving on as soon as we've finished."

Cramarc and Agninga were already getting some of the supplies down from the cart. Luckily the gnomes weren't too fussy when it came to food as the bread had started to go mouldy in the tunnel and the vegetables were going off a bit as well. Despite this, the gnomes were so hungry that they wolfed down whatever was put in front of them and washed it down with refreshing draughts of cool water from a nearby stream.

"Everybody finished?" Asked Cramarc.

"Can we rest for a while?" Asked Pullup. "I don't think my legs could move another step."

"We can't rest here in case the elves come, but we will have a long stop as soon as we can find somewhere safe," said Romanamor.

The family was all very weary by this time, as they had just travelled for a day and a half without a break. However the effort had to be made to move on.

"Right let's go," said Tromort. "If we don't move now, we never will."

So the exhausted family made their first tentative steps into Humanland. It was their equivalent of man's first step on the moon.

"Which direction shall we go in?" Asked Cramarc.

"I don't suppose it makes any difference, as we don't know where we're going anyway," said Romanamor.

They decided to just carry on in a straight line away from the tunnel and see where they ended up.

The going was fairly easy as they were on a downhill slope and were able to push the cart with very little effort. They had not been travelling for too long when they came to a wooded area that they thought would be the ideal place to stop for a rest. This area was not really far enough away from the tunnel for the gnomes to feel completely safe, but they were so tired that they decided to take a chance and stop there anyway.

The trees in the wood were quite close together, and the gnomes didn't have to travel too far in to be hidden from view.

"I'll take the first watch if you like," volunteered Tromort.

"That's fine by me," said Romanamor. "I'll take the second."

"I think I'll stay with Tromort," said Agninga. "He's likely to fall asleep, but the two of us can keep each other awake."

It was agreed by all of them that she should stay with her husband. The rest of the gnomes settled down and within a short while their loud snoring could be heard echoing around the woods.

Tromort and Agninga found a place to sit and although they were both totally worn out, managed to stop each other from dozing off. They watched the sun slowly moving across the sky and they knew instinctively when it was time to awaken Romanamor for the second watch.

"Is it time for me to wake up already?" He yawned. "Anything happen while I was asleep?"

"All seems very quiet," said Tromort. "Will you be able to stay awake on your own or shall I waken Cramarc?"

"No that's all right, let her sleep, I have a thousand and one things to think about to keep me awake," said Romanamor.

So Romanamor took up Tromort and Agninga's position and settled down for his vigil. The snoring volume increased as Tromort and Agninga immediately fell into a deep sleep.

Romanamor was still very tired and try as he may, he couldn't keep his eyes open, and very soon he was snoring away with the others. He was just falling into the very deepest sleep possible when he was awakened by a strange tinkling sound. This sound was followed by some of the most frightening sounds he had ever heard. They started off as low moans and became gradually louder.

Mmerrooo! The noises seemed to be saying. Romanamor hid behind one of the trees, the noises got increasingly louder, whatever it was, was getting closer. Then he saw them, huge black and white monsters with large horns and funny bits dangling underneath. Romanamor was petrified, and the only reason he didn't actually go solid was because he had swallowed a good dose of potion before he had started his watch.

What should he do? Wake the others or wait and see what these monsters were going to do?

The more he looked, the more he realised that these creatures, despite their huge size, didn't actually look aggressive.

He decided to wake Tromort anyway as he felt he needed a second opinion.

"Wwwhat's the matter?" Asked Tromort.

"Creatures," whispered Romanamor. "Stol fo meht."

"Would you mind calming down a bit, I can't understand a word you're saying," said Tromort, firmly.

Romanamor sat down and began slowly nodding his head. After a few minutes he began to feel calmer, and he felt his brain slipping into forwards gear once again.

"Creatures," he said. "Lots of them."

"Where?" Asked Tromort, looking worried.

"Walking past just at the edge of the woods, huge black and white things," stammered Romanamor.

"Sounds like some cows to me," said Tromort casually.

"Some what?" Queried Romanamor.

"Cows," came the reply. "They're quite harmless, all they do is eat grass all day."

"How do you know about them?" Asked Romanamor.

"A great uncle of mine told me. He was a very brave adventurer, and he couldn't resist the challenge of going through the tunnel."

"How come you never mentioned him before?" Asked Romanamor.

"Well, the rest of my family thought he was mad. The young gnomes were told to keep quiet about him as they didn't want anyone to think there was madness in the family," said Tromort.

"So if he was mad, why did you believe what he told you?"

"I was a very young gnome and believed everything I heard, anyway I didn't think he was mad, I thought he was a hero," said Tromort, defensively.

"Did he tell you anything else about Humanland?" Questioned Romanamor.

"Not much," said Tromort. "He may have been very brave, but even he didn't dare venture too far into Humanland."

"So these cow creatures aren't dangerous?" Said Romanamor

"No, definitely not," stressed Tromort.

"I think it's time then, that we woke the others and continued on our way," said Romanamor.

When they had awakened the other gnomes, Romanamor and Tromort explained to them all about the cows so that they wouldn't be scared when they saw them.

"Nevertheless," warned Romanamor. "We'd better have another dose of the potion as we don't know what else we're going to come across."

"We'd better have something to eat before we go. Unfortunately there's only vegetables as the bread has gone very mouldy," apologised Cramarc, even though it wasn't her fault.

"Oh well, just vegetables it is then," sighed Romanamor, gnawing at a rather large carrot.

"Very nice too," said Tromort, getting stuck into a slightly going off cabbage. "I always think they taste better when they're a bit over-ripe."

"They're a bit more than over-ripe, these vegetables are on the point of being completely rotten," said Agninga, "I think we have to start looking for fresh food as we travel."

After eating what they could of the rotting food, the brave little gnomes set off. Everything looked much the same as in Gnomeland, apart from the cows of course. They were travelling down a slope into a large valley and it took the combined strength of Romanamor and Tromort to prevent the cart from rolling down the hill all by itself.

Everyone was in quite a buoyant mood. After all, they had got through the tunnel unscathed and there was no sign of the elves anywhere.

Gnomes are natural gatherers of food, Pullup and Tippit were walking either side of the convoy collecting a variety of berries and plants that they knew were safe for gnomes to eat. They passed lots more cows on the way that occasionally looked up but were generally far too busy munching the lush grass to take much notice of the passing gnomes.

There were just a few hours of daylight left and the gnomes wanted to put as much distance between themselves and the mountains as possible. Progress became easier as the sloping ground began to level off, and there were more shrubs and trees to take cover in, should the need arise.

The rest of the day passed with no new surprises. Pullup and Tippit had managed to gather enough food for a meal, albeit a very small one. The gnomes found a grassy clearing in the middle of a small area of woodland where they felt it would be safe to rest for the night. Cramarc and Agninga offered to take the first watch, as Tromort and Romanamor looked completely worn out. The male gnomes readily agreed to this idea, provided that if anything untoward happened, they were woken immediately. Tippit and Pullup were already fast asleep, huddled together under a large beech tree.

"We'll get some sleep too now, if that's alright with you?" Yawned Romanamor.

"But remember, you must wake us up at the slightest sign of a disturbance."

"Don't worry, we will," said the females together.

Romanamor and Tromort were snoring away before their heads hit the soft ground. As the night drew on, Cramarc and Agninga became increasingly nervous. The occasional fox or badger could be heard moving through the undergrowth, an owl landed on a nearby branch and it's hooting was a comforting, friendly sound to the two gnomes as they sat staring into the darkness. They decided to let the males sleep on, and they both managed to keep their vigil going all though the night, one or the other of them occasionally dozing off, but awakening quickly at the thought that something might happen. Dawn seemed a long time coming for Cramarc and Agninga, but eventually the first chinks of sunlight began to appear on the distant horizon.

Romanamor and Tippit woke at the first signs of daylight. Years of working in their vegetable gardens from dawn until dusk had conditioned them to waking up as soon as it began getting light. Pullup and Tippit, however had to be woken by Cramarc.

"Come on children," she urged. "We must be on our way as soon as possible."

Pullup and Tippit moaned a bit at being wakened so early in the morning, but they realised the urgency in their mother's voice and were soon up and about. There was a small stream nearby and the gnomes gave their faces a good splashing to wake themselves up properly. They were able to replenish their water supply and Tippit had found some wild strawberries in the woods. The gnomes were starting to feel hungry by now.

"We must find some more food soon," said Tromort. "I don't know how long I can continue on a nearly-empty stomach."

"I wonder just how far it is to the place these humans live," remarked Cramarc.

"Not too far, I hope," replied Romanamor. "I'm sure we'll find some signs of human life before long."

"Human life and food," said Tromort, still thinking about his rumbling tummy.

"Right everybody, ready, let's go," urged Cramarc, not wanting to waste a second of precious daylight hours.

So they set off, not hurrying, but at the steady gnome pace, that could keep them going all day long, without over-tiring themselves. It was about mid-morning, when they came across something very strange, well very strange to gnomes anyway. To them it was a wide strip of hard grey stuff that seemed to go on forever in both directions, humans call it a road. Romanamor was quick to realise what it could be.

"It must be what the humans use to travel on, to get to another village," he said emphatically.

"Why don't they just use tracks like we do? Asked Cramarc.

"How should I know? I've never been here before either," answered Romanamor.

"They must have very big carts to need a track this size," pondered Tromort. "What if one comes along while we're stood here?"

They soon got their answer. It started off as a distant noise and grew louder as it got closer.

"Quick, into the bushes," said Tromort.

The noise soon became a roar. The gnomes had just got themselves hidden when a big blue, four-wheeled cart rushed past making more noise than the gnomes had ever heard in their lives. It was just as well that the gnomes were taking their doses of potion or they would have gone solid there and then. A few seconds later another one rushed past, this time a red one.

"Tahw era yeht?" Asked a panicking Agninga.

"Ev'I on aedi," answered Tromort, also going into backwards speech.

"Tub I kniht d'ew retteb peek tuo fo rieht yaw."

"Emoc no!" Said Romanamor, rapidly nodding his head. "Come on, snap out of it, I don't think we'll be harmed, so long as we keep out of their way."

Chapter 6

Rescuing the First Gnome

The gnomes set off cautiously, staying well out of sight. They could still hear the cars rushing past, so they knew they were walking parallel to the road.

"I wonder how far it is to the nearest village?" Pondered Cramarc to herself.

Pullup and Tippit continued their foraging, being careful not to stray too close to the road. They walked for miles and miles before they came upon any signs of humans, apart from the road that is. They came across a small cottage tucked away in the woods, surrounded by a well-tended garden. There was a small pond in the corner and there, sat by the edge, fishing rod in hand, was the most life-like garden gnome you're ever likely to see. The gnomes moved through the woods around the edge of the garden, until they were next to the pond.

"He's definitely one of us," whispered Romanamor.

"You can see it in his eyes," said Cramarc

"He looks almost alive," commented Pullup.

There were no signs of humans in the garden, but the gnomes were not sure whether there were any humans in the house.

"We'd better wait until it starts getting dark," suggested Romanamor.

So the gnomes settled down for a while, waiting for darkness to fall. They had a small snack of hazelnuts that Tippit and Pullup had found a little while earlier. These were washed down with some water and a dose of the potion. It wasn't long before it started becoming dark. Unfortunately there was a full moon, and it didn't get as dark as the gnomes had hoped.

"We'll have to try and rescue him anyway," said Romanamor. "One of us is going to have to take a chance."

"Maybe I should go," suggested Pullup. "Being smaller, there's less chance of me being seen."

There still were no signs of life in the cottage, so Cramarc agreed that it would be a good idea for Pullup to go. Tromort handed Pullup a mug of the potion.

"Be very careful lad," he warned. "If anyone comes, just keep very, very still."

"If he is a real gnome and not one of the copies, you'll need to lay him down so that as much of the potion as possible goes into his mouth," whispered Romanamor.

"Because he may take a while to recover, I suggest that you take his place at the pond until he does so."

"Good luck," whispered Cramarc.

The fence around the garden was old and falling to bits, and there were a few gaps where a small gnome could easily get through. Pullup climbed through the gap nearest to the pond and moved slowly through the flowerbed towards it. When he got to the gnome, he tipped it over very gently and dragged it back from its position. He put his hand in the mug and dabbed a few drops of potion on its lips. There were no signs of life, so he dabbed on some more potion and then remembering what his dad had said, he grabbed the fishing rod and sat next to the pond, trying to look as unreal as possible. It was just as well he did, because as he sat down, there was a roar from the road and some very bright lights came through the woods towards the cottage. The bright lights swung round into the drive next to the cottage, lighting up the whole garden. Pullup did his best to stay still but he couldn't help closing his eyes when they were dazzled by the lights. After what seemed like forever, the roaring stopped and the lights went out. The gnomes could hear the humans talking excitedly, as they got out of the cart. Soon afterwards a light went on in the cottage. The garden was lit up, although not quite so brightly as before. Meanwhile the gnome behind Pullup was starting to show signs of life. He raised his head slowly, a look of total bewilderment on his face. He had no recollection of anything that had happened to him. He had gone to bed in Gnomeland and woken up here in this strange place.

"Try and keep still," said Pullup. "If it goes dark again, make a run for that fence over there."

"Yako," said the traumatised gnome.

It was quite a while before the humans turned out the lights in the cottage, and Pullup was finding it difficult keeping up the pose with the fishing rod, but eventually everything went dark and he could relax his arms.

"Make a run for the fence," he whispered, glancing over his shoulder.

The gnome wasn't capable of running, his legs were stiff because they had been in the same position for so long, but he managed a sort of fast stagger towards where the other gnomes were waiting.

"Welcome back to the land of the living," said Romanamor.

Ev'I syawla neeb ni eht dnal fo eht gnivil. I saw erawa fo gnihtyreve taht saw gnineppah tub I t'ndluoc nur yawa. Eht sevle dekcip em pu. Sevle! Sevle!" He suddenly shouted, panicking.

"It's all right, it's all right, there are no elves here, only us," assured Agninga, putting her arm protectively round him.

"Can you remember what your name is?" Asked Agninga.

"Gnihtemos ekil Grattarg," he answered.

"I think the first priority is to get you speaking forwards again so we can understand what you're saying," said Romanamor. "Try nodding your head up and down."

Grattarg did so, very slowly at first because his neck was stiff, but as the muscles got looser his head nodded faster.

"All right you can stop now. That should have done the trick," ordered Romanamor.

"That's better," said Grattarg. "My head feels back to normal now."

"Good," sighed Romanamor. "And now I would like to explain exactly what we are doing here."

Romanamor just gave Grattarg a brief outline of their adventure so far.

"I must be the first gnome you've rescued, then," said Grattarg.

"Yes, and just rescuing one gnome makes it all worthwhile," smiled Cramarc.

"Hadn't we better be making a move?" Asked Tromort, getting anxious that the absence of Grattarg might be discovered.

"Is everyone ready?" Asked Romanamor.

Everyone said that they were and they began to move off towards the road again. Grattarg was struggling to keep up, his legs not yet fully recovered.

"Why don't we let Grattarg ride on the cart? There's plenty of room now that most of the supplies are gone." Suggested Cramarc.

They all agreed that this would be the best thing to do for the time being, and they set off again with Grattarg on the cart.

Grattarg was quite philosophical about the way he had been treated since coming to Humanland. "The humans were very good to me and showed me a lot of respect. I fell in the pond a few times, and they were very quick to get me out and put me on dry land again."

On a lighter note, he joked that although he had been in that position for so many years, he had still not yet caught a fish. The other gnomes laughed when he said this.

"At least you've still got a sense of humour," said Tippit. "I'm sure I'd have been very miserable after being stuck in one position for so many years."

"The most upsetting thing is all those wasted years and I really missed my mum and dad. In fact, I often wonder if they're still alive."

"So you can actually remember the times that you fell into the pond?" Asked Tromort.

"Quite distinctly," answered Grattarg.

"So even if you cannot move, you are still aware of what's going on around you?" Asked Romanamor.

"Yes," said Grattarg. "But no matter how hard I try, I still can't move my body. How did you manage it?"

Tromort went on to explain about the reason for their trip to Humanland and about the magic properties of the potion.

"Can I stay with you and help you find the others?" Asked Grattarg.

"Of course you can," said Romanamor. "The more gnomes we have involved with the search, the more chance we have of finding some more."

The Gnomes had covered some distance between themselves and the cottage, but they decided to continue throughout the night. They passed a few cottages on the way and always had a good look in the gardens to see if there were any gnomes in them. A couple of the gardens contained gnomes, but on closer inspection, they were only the dull replicas made by the humans. In the hour before dawn they decided to start looking for a safe place to hide during the day.

Pullup and Tippit had been foraging for food during the night, but alas, had not been able to find anything that looked remotely edible.

"We must find some food soon," moaned Tromort. "I can't keep going for much longer on an empty stomach."

"It's very difficult looking for food in the dark," said Tippit defensively.

"No one's blaming you," comforted Cramarc. "What we really need to find is a cottage where the humans like growing vegetables."

Their thoughts on food were answered shortly afterwards. They came to a small stretch of woodland next to the road, and just beyond it there was a large field full of cabbages.

"Perfect," said Tromort. "Somewhere safe to stay for the day and a whole field full of food."

Tromort rubbed his empty stomach in expectation.

"I don't think I can wait until it gets dark again. Maybe we can sneak over and get a couple of cabbages without being seen."

They were all extremely hungry by now and desperate times call for desperate measures. Pullup and Tippit were designated to collect some cabbages as they were the smallest and therefore the least likely to be detected. The young gnomes were understandably very nervous about doing this and Cramarc gave them a spoonful of potion each to give them more courage.

Pullup and Tippit crawled over to where the cabbages were, picked two each and then ran back to where the others were anxiously waiting. Emboldened by what they had just done, they wanted to go back for some more.

Romanamor stopped them. "No point in risking detection any more than is absolutely necessary," he said. "Four cabbages between us are quite enough for now. We can get some more when it becomes dark."

Raw cabbage isn't exactly the ideal food, but to the starving gnomes it was like a banquet and they consumed the makeshift meal with relish. Almost full now and fairly confident that they were well hidden in the woods, the gnomes settled down for a well-deserved sleep. Within a short while, the sound of their snoring mixed with woodland birdsong, were the only sounds to be heard.

Chapter 7

Return of the Elves

The Gnomes were content for the time being, but all was far from safe. The elves had returned in large numbers to the tunnel entrance. They used diversionary tactics to get the builders out of the way and then the bulk of the elves, led by Snitchmire and Prodlife bundled their way into the tunnel. By the time the builders realised that they had been fooled, it was too late and there was no way they could stop the elves from going through. There were nearly 100 elves altogether and it wouldn't be long before they were through the tunnel and hot on the trail of the family.

The elves had been in Humanland many times before, and it gave them a big advantage over the gnomes. They knew where to find food and where all the best hiding places were, and of course they weren't slowed down, as the gnomes were, by having a cart to push. The only thing in the gnomes' favour was the fact that they were three days ahead of their enemies.

The gnomes slept blissfully on, unaware that the elves were already beginning to pick up their trail. The elves were using their keen sense of smell to pick up the scent of the gnomes, much the same as bloodhounds do in the human world. The gnomes have a very distinctive scent and if the wind was blowing in the right direction, the elves could pick it up over long distances.

The elves were very cunning, especially when it came to strategies of war, and they realised that 100 elves together would find it very difficult to stay hidden. They solved this by splitting up into smaller groups and used runners to keep each group informed as to what was going on. Like the gnomes, the elves decided it would only be safe to travel at night.

Back in Gnomeland, the builders, realising that they had been conned by the elves, decided that everything possible must be done to protect Romanamor, Cramarc and the rest of the adventurers. Two of the builders went back to Stonemarble to try and organise some help. They managed to persuade a couple of their builder friends that it was necessary to try and find Frogorf as they desperately needed some more of the potion. These particular builders were willing to help in any way they could and not only did they say they would find Frogorf, but they would deliver the potion straight to Grassroot. They also managed to persuade other builders that building was of secondary importance to protecting the family, and with 25 or so volunteers in tow, they set off back towards the tunnel.

Granarg, meanwhile, had led the rest of the builders through the tunnel and had begun following the trail of the elves. One of them was carrying the flagon of potion, which, although half empty, might still come in very useful. Because there was only half of the potion left, they agreed that it should only be used in an emergency.

"I hope they find Frogorf, this potion really is magical stuff," said Roccor.

"And very necessary magical stuff at that," agreed Granarg. "Without it I doubt whether any of us would have got as far as we have."

"I wonder how far the family have got?" Mused Roccor.

"Let's hope they're still alive and well," said Granarg.

The builders fell silent now, concentrating their efforts into walking as fast as possible, spurred on by the thought that the family would be in real danger if the elves got to them first.

Chapter 8

Finding Naggan

Further on in Humanland, the family was now awake and they were just sat around waiting for darkness to fall, so that they could be on their way. They were all sitting down, that is, except Grattarg, who was pacing up and down, trying to get the stiffness out of his legs. He wanted to help the others and he realised that he could be of more use if he was mobile.

"How do you feel now, young lad?" Asked Romanamor.

"My legs are still aching, but I think I will be able to walk tonight instead of riding on the cart."

"Brave fellow," said Tromort. "I think it's amazing that you can be so strong-willed after all those years in the same position."

"It's after being in that place for so long, that makes me realise how bad it must be for the others. I want to help them in the same way that you helped me," said Grattarg sincerely.

"You can help us forage for food if you feel up to it," said Tippit.

"I'll try," said Grattarg. "But at the moment it takes all my effort just to put one leg in front of the other."

Cramarc was watching the sun sink slowly down towards the horizon.

"I think we could risk making a move now," she said.

"Yes, I think it would be safe, but we must pick a few cabbages first," said Romanamor.

No sooner said than done, thought Tippit and Pullup. They rushed straight over into the field and began picking. They came back with armfuls and were all set to go and get some more.

"We don't need too many," said Cramarc. "They'll only go off if we keep them for too long."

"Do you think we've got enough then?" Asked Pullup.

"Yes, they should last us for a couple of days," said Romanamor. "And now we'd better be on our way."

They checked that everything on the cart was secure and left the sanctuary of the woods, moving into open space once again. They had to be extra cautious until it became completely dark and even then, did not stray too close to the road for fear of being caught in the car headlights.

They were passing more and more cottages now, and they carefully checked the gardens of each one, alas to no avail.

"The human village can't be far now; do you think we could stop and have something to eat before we get there?" Asked Tromort, who seemed to get hungry long before anyone else did.

Quite a few of the gardens had vegetables growing in them and Tippit and Pullup had managed to gather a variety of different foods.

"Do you realise we're doing exactly the same as the elves?" Said Agninga, crunching into a large carrot. "We're turning into a bunch of thieves."

"I suppose we are stealing, but we're only doing it to keep ourselves alive and not because we are too lazy to grow our own food like the elves," explained Tromort.

Stolen or not, the food was still consumed with relish by the hungry gnomes. They were on their way as soon as they'd finished eating. Grattarg was moving a lot more freely now and was easily keeping up with the others. They weren't walking for very long when they realised that the cottages were much closer together than before, some were in small clusters of eight or 10, others were lined up fairly dose together along the main street.

"This must be it," said Tromort. "We've finally reached the village."

"This probably isn't the only village in Humanland, there must be a few more scattered around, don't you think?" Said Romanamor.

"But this one will do to start with," replied Tromort.

"Right. Now, we can't just go marching around the village willy-nilly, we need to plan things out a bit first," said Romanamor.

"We need to find somewhere to hide the cart," said Cramarc.

They all agreed that they would be able to move around more freely without the cart, and after searching for a while, they came across an old disused barn.

"Perfect," said Romanamor. "Looks like a good place for us to hide for the day as well."

The barn had obviously been neglected for a long time and there were large holes in the roof, but it was the ideal place for the gnomes to hide. It was also a good place to send rescued gnomes to, if they should find any. There was still a couple of hours of darkness left and the gnomes decided to have a scout around the area to see what was what.

"We'd better take a small flagon of potion with us in case we come across any solid gnomes," suggested Cramarc.

"Good idea," said Romanamor. "And I think we'd better have a dose each before we go, we don't know what we might come across."

With the cart safely hidden away, the gnomes set off and began their search. Pullup and Tippit were searching a little bit away from the main group, and it was them who discovered the first of the gardens with gnomes in. The humans who lived in this cottage had obviously developed a great liking for gnomes. There were gnomes in every conceivable pose, pushing wheel-barrows, fishing, using various garden implements, lying down, sitting up or just standing there like sentries watching over the garden.

"They all look pretty life-like to me," said Romanamor. "But it's getting a bit near to daytime to start rescuing any."

All of a sudden Agninga became very excited, everyone looked, to see what she was getting so worked up about.

"I can't really tell from this distance, but that one over there certainly looks like Naggan."

"Where?" Asked Tromort.

"Lying down, over on the other side, I must go and have a closer look."

"I'll come with you," said Tromort. "But we'll have to be very careful not to be seen."

"Can we take some potion with us, just in case it is him?" Asked Agninga.

"If it is Naggan I should think it's alright to rescue him now. After all, there are so many gnomes here that I don't think one would be missed," said Romanamor.

So Agninga and Tromort crept across the semi-dark garden over to where the gnome they thought was Naggan, lay.

"It's definitely him," whispered Agninga, tears of joy beginning to trickle down her cheeks.

Naggan was already on his back so administering the potion was fairly easy.

"We can't wait here for much longer," said Tromort. "We'd better carry him over to safety."

They picked up their son and carried him back to where the others were waiting. Cramarc was barely able to hide her disappointment that it wasn't Potstop.

"Don't fret my dear," comforted Romanamor. "I'm sure we're going to find Potstop soon."

Naggan meanwhile, was coming round.

"Erehw ma I?" Were the first words that he uttered.

"It's all right my son, you're safe now," Tromort whispered.

The shock of hearing Tromort's voice was enough to change the direction of the words in Naggan's spiral brain.

"Dad, Mum! I never thought I'd see you again," said Naggan.

"However did you find me?"

With a lot of effort and a lot of luck," said a still sobbing Agninga. They decided that further explanation could wait until Naggan was fully recovered.

"We'd better be making our way back to the old barn now," urged Romanamor.

Tromort decided that it would easier to carry Naggan until he'd got some of the stiffness out of his legs. They arrived back at the barn just as the sun was beginning to peek its way over the horizon.

"We're going to have to wait until nightfall before rescuing the others," stated Romanamor.

"I don't mind relaxing for the day, I'm completely worn out," said Cramarc.

The gnomes had a quick meal washed down with some water from a nearby stream, it was a bit muddy, but the gnomes needed a drink and it would have to suffice until something better come along.

Chapter 9

Elves and Builders

A bit further back in Humanland, the elves were making fairly fast progress. Not as fast as the builders, however, who had been marching army style throughout the night and were actually catching them up. One of the smaller groups of elves were dragging their heels and were consequently a long way behind the main group. They were having a great time. They were raiding the gardens and breaking into the occasional cottage if there was no evidence of occupation.

The builders were aware that they were gaining on this small band of elves; they could hear the occasional cackle from somewhere up ahead.

After hearing the cackles, the builders made sure that they travelled in absolute silence. They stopped for a moment and because they knew that confrontation with the elves was imminent, all had an extra-large swig of the magic potion.

"Listen," whispered Granarg, "This is our first encounter with the elves, since we arrived in Humanland, let's get it right."

"How many do you think there are?" Asked one of the builders nervously.

"Bit hard to tell, we'll just have to take a chance that there aren't too many," whispered Granarg.

"What we need to do is tie them up so that they can't cause any trouble."

Builders were very good at always carrying things around that might come in handy, and they had brought the rope with them that they had used to help the family across the river.

"Let's make a move then," said Granarg in a low voice. "And remember, we don't want to scare them off, just catch them by surprise."

The builders moved off at quite a fast pace and were soon within earshot of the elves once more. The elves were behaving very noisily and their cackling laughter could be heard quite clearly. They had been drinking some of the funny tasting liquid that one of the elves had stolen from a nearby cottage. They had all developed a taste for this particular liquid and it was party time whenever they could get their hands on any.

The fact that the elves were becoming very drunk, gave the builders a big advantage because the elfin revelry meant that they were entirely oblivious to anything else that was going on. The more noise they made, the less chance they had of hearing the approaching builders. They were surrounded before they realised what was happening.

"There's someone out there," said one of the laughing elves.

"No there isn't," said another one. "It's just your stupid brain imagining things."

"Shut up, Squiggly. I thought I heard something as well," hissed another one.

"So did I."

"And me."

Went a chorus of drunken agreement.

"Well, there's nothing out there that could possibly bother us," sneered Squiggly.

"You're right for once in your stupid life. It was probably just a fox or badger anyway."

But it wasn't a fox, or a badger, it was 18 very large, very brave builder gnomes who had decided that now was the best time to attack.

Granarg led the assault, closely followed by the others. It was easier than the gnomes had anticipated because the elves were very drunk and disorientated, in fact they weren't really aware of what was happening at all. The builders managed to grab all of the elves except for two. These two were not quite as drunk as the others and had managed to pick up the sharp, pointed sticks that were the main weapon of the elves. They went into a slightly crouched position and began jabbing the sticks in the general direction of the builders. Being dark, it was very hit or miss with the sticks, and the builders managed to elude them quite easily. The elves did, however, stab one of the builders in the arm.

"Why you little!" Shouted the builder, getting very angry and moving towards the elf responsible.

"Don't get too close," warned Granarg. "They can be quite dangerous if you get too close."

"Just keep their attention for a while," said Roccor, who then moved off to one side motioning to one of the other builders to follow him as he did so. They circled around the elves with the pointed sticks and moving silently, grasped them from behind. Despite the elves wriggling, the gnomes managed to overcome them and made them drop their pointed sticks, which fell with a clatter onto the ground.

"Well done!" Congratulated Granarg. "Now let's get them tied up and be on our way."

There was more than enough rope to tie the elves' hands and feet together. They then looped the rope twice around a large pine tree and tied it as tightly as they could. Granarg checked that the knots were secure, knowing that the elves, with their devious ways of doing things, were unlikely to stay tied up for very long.

"Good," he said, when he was fully satisfied. "Let's be on our way."

They set off at quite a fast pace, following the trail of the other elves. Capturing the drunken elves had given the builders a new confidence in their ability to succeed in their mission.

"We could never have done it without the potion," pointed out Granarg.

"We'll have to be careful from now on as we haven't got that much left, we'd better save it for times when we really need it."

"Won't be easy," said Toocoot. "I'm getting to like this feeling of boldness."

"We'll have to learn to be brave without the potion," answered Granarg.

"We'd better start looking for somewhere to hide for the day," said Roccor.

"Agreed," said Granarg.

The night was beginning to turn from pitch black to the misty-grey shade of dawn and the gnomes managed to find a nice little wooded copse that they thought would be the ideal place to spend the day resting, without being disturbed. They had brought some food with them and had gathered more on the way. There was enough for quite a substantial meal, which they ate before settling down for a hard-earned rest. Although they had been full of beans at the time, the events of the night had taken more energy than they realised and it wasn't long before the builders were all fast asleep.

A few miles further on, the other elves were also finding somewhere to hide and at the same time the family were settling down for the day in the disused barn.

Chapter 10

Frogorf Decides to Go

The builders back in Gnomeland did not have to worry about not moving around in the daytime and were achieving their particular aims very quickly indeed. Four of them had taken one of the large builders' carts and had made their way up through the Grey Wood. At this very moment they were discussing with Frogorf the urgent need for more potion. Frogorf was very happy to see the potion being put to such good use and willingly let the builders load as much as was needed onto the cart.

"The outcome of this mission is very important to me," he said. "And I will do everything in my power to make sure you succeed."

The thought going through Frogorf's mind at the moment was, should he be going with the builders? Was he doing everything in his power to help them if he just stayed in his cave? Was he acting cowardly again like he did all those years ago? He thought long and hard until finally he reached a decision.

"I hope you don't mind," he said. "But I really must come with you. I couldn't live with myself if I just stayed here and everything went wrong."

"Of course we don't mind, the more gnomes we have on our side the better," said one of the builders.

"Good, let's be off then. I'll push the cart if you like," said Frogorf, wanting to be helpful.

The builders were very grateful for any help they could get and agreed readily to let Frogorf push the cart.

"We'll take over when you get tired," assured the builders.

Frogorf's sheer size made the cart look fairly small in comparison, and the builders realised that he would be able to push the cart for quite a long way before he got weary.

They had arranged to meet the rest of the builders back in Grassroot. Taffat had taken it on himself to go to Stonemarble and recruit as many volunteers as possible to accompany him back to Grassroot. All building and repair work was suspended for a while, as nearly all of the builders wanted to go with Taffat. The only ones who didn't go were the very old ones who thought that the journey would be too much for them.

When they finally all met up in Grassroot, there was a grand total of 29 builders, 30 if you include Frogorf. Quite a formidable little army thought Taffat, pleased with himself that he had been able to get so many volunteers. Wasting no time at all, they gathered as much food as they could carry from the main food store and piled it, along with some fresh water, onto the cart that they had brought with them.

Frogorf was still very much in awe of the fact that he was finally back among his fellow gnomes. He was very quiet and kept out of the way whilst the rest of them were loading the supplies.

The builders, in turn, were in awe of Frogorf, mainly because of his great size. One hundred and eighty years of hammering and chiselling had given him muscles twice the size of any of the builders.

The cart was loaded in no time at all, and they were soon ready to move off in the direction of the tunnel. They decided it would be a good idea to leave Frogorf in charge of the potion, as he was the one who had developed it. They started off at a steady pace, the builders pushing the supply cart at the front and Frogorf bringing up the rear with the cart containing the flagons of potion. Builders were naturally slow movers, but they had great stamina and could keep going for extraordinary lengths of time. They would probably be in Humanland before they needed a rest.

Chapter 11

Continuing The Rescue

In Humanland itself, darkness was falling and Romanamor and the other gnomes in the barn were wide-awake, planning their next move.

"There must be nearly 20 gnomes in the garden," said Romanamor.

"If they all just disappear, they will definitely be missed."

Cramarc came up with a good idea. "Why don't we rescue them and then tell them to stay in their original positions for a day, so that we can be well away by the time their disappearance is discovered?"

"Excellent idea," agreed Romanamor. "I shouldn't think they'd mind doing that, if it meant that they could escape safely."

"Settled then!" Said Tromort emphatically. "We might as well do it now, then we give ourselves as much time as possible to get away."

The humans were still moving around in the house and the gnomes had to be very careful not to be seen. They moved stealthily from gnome to gnome, administering the potion. There was one scary moment when a large female human came out of the back door, but all she did was put a large bag full of something into a metal container. When this happened, all the gnomes stood as still as possible, so that if the human glanced up towards the garden, there was a good chance that they would not be noticed. When the human had gone back inside, they carried on reviving the stiff gnomes, telling them as they did so, to remain in their positions. Soon all of the solid gnomes had been given a dose of the potion and the family retreated back to the edge of the garden.

"I think we got all of them," said Romanamor, looking across the garden and trying to memorise reviving each one. Satisfied at last, he motioned to the others to begin moving towards the rest of the village. They travelled in silence until they got well clear of the house.

Naggan, as you can imagine, was full of questions, but he waited until they were in the clear before he started asking any. How did his mum and dad get there? How did they revive him? Who were the others?

Agninga did her best to explain everything to him as they travelled along. She decided not to tell him about the elves knowing what was going on, until he had fully recovered from his ordeal.

The gnomes moved silently on, taking care that they only walked along the back of the gardens and not too near the actual houses. Dogs, which would normally have barked at intruders, seemed to ignore the gnomes, probably because the scent they picked up was the same as the scent on some of the harmless statues that sat in the gardens.

They found the occasional gnome that needed rescuing, and made sure that the recovering gnomes knew to stay where they were for at least a day, to give the family a chance to get away.

The gnomes stopped to rest near a large silent building. It was a massive structure with a tower at one end and a huge wooden door halfway along the side. They felt quite safe here, as there didn't seem to be any sign of humans. Just across the road, however, was a building that seemed to be bursting with life. Lots of humans appeared to be enjoying themselves inside and there were sounds of talking and laughter. In the background there was the sound of music. Alongside the building, there was a large garden and some of the humans were sitting around wooden tables, eating and drinking. All around the garden were gnomes in every conceivable position. They were too far away for the family to work out if they were real gnomes, or just the reproduction ones made by humans.

"We can't possibly rescue any of these gnomes with all the humans about," Romanamor sighed. "I wonder if they ever go home to bed?"

"We'd better just wait here and see," Tromort answered. "If they are real gnomes, we can't just abandon them."

So the family sat and rested for a while, glad in a way, of any respite they could get. Pullup, Tippit and Naggan, being younger were full of energy and couldn't wait to carry on with the mission but they sat down quietly with the adults, respect for their elders overcoming the urge to be active.

After waiting for what seemed an eternity, the humans began coming out of the door, still making as much noise as they did when they were inside. A few cars started up and could be heard driving off in either direction. Among the last to leave was a man on his own, who was obviously very drunk. He staggered around the doorway for a while and then staggered across the road towards the church.

"Keep very quiet and very still," whispered Cramarc, as the drunk human come lurching into the churchyard.

The man was so drunk that he'd lost all sense of direction and continued wandering up the church path near to the gnomes. Although the gnomes kept very still, they did not have time to hide themselves properly, and the drunk man spied them, crouching down by the church wall.

"Aha!" He said. "What have we here then? Gnomes if I'm very much not mistaken. Now why has the vicar begun bringing gnomes into the churchyard? They don't belong here; this is a place of worship. I must have a word with the vicar in the morning and get them moved." Talking to himself about the gnomes seemed to sober him up a bit and he walked unsteadily back out into the street, where I imagine he managed to find his way home, eventually.

When he did tell the vicar in the morning, he become the butt of one of the best jokes in the village for years. When the vicar went to look for the gnomes, he didn't find any and everyone who met the drunk after the incident would ask him if he'd seen any gnomes lately.

In the end he began to doubt his own mind and decided to give up drinking altogether, before he got into any more trouble.

Once the drunk human had gone, it was at least another hour before the lights had all gone out in the house opposite.

"Right, let's make a move then," whispered Romanamor. 'We can leave the cart here and just carry a flagon with us."

They moved as silently and as quickly as they could, crossing the road one at a time to lessen the chances of being detected, should one of the humans be looking from a window in the darkened house.

They all reached the garden safely and began looking more closely at the still gnomes. The garden was fairly large and each of the family checked out a different section. When they'd finished checking they met up in the corner of the garden furthest away from the house.

"Most of them seem to be real," whispered Tromort.

"That's true," said Romanamor. "We'd better give all of them a dose to make sure we don't miss any out."

"Any sign of Potstop?" Asked Cramarc anxiously.

"I haven't seen him," said Romanamor.

"Neither have we," said Pullup and Tippit sadly.

"Don't worry," sympathised Agninga. "You're bound to find him sooner or later."

"I'm sure we will, but for now we'd better concentrate on rescuing the ones that are here," said Romanamor.

They each took a small mug and began reviving the gnomes in the sections they had checked. If any human had looked out of the window, they would have witnessed a very strange sight indeed. Live gnomes walking amongst their garden ones, tilting them backwards and giving them a drink. As it turned out, in the end, only about half of the gnomes were real and the rest were just very good reproductions.

When they'd finished, they met up again in the far corner of the garden.

"Some of the gnomes are so life-like it's almost impossible to tell the difference," sighed Romanamor.

"In daylight we could probably tell them apart," said Cramarc. "It does seem a shame to waste all that potion on false gnomes."

"Did you recognise any of them?" Asked Tromort.

"I'm sure I used to know a couple of them when I was younger," said Tippit. "There were two brothers who lived on the other side of the village, we used to play with them sometimes."

"I know who you mean," said Pullup. "They both disappeared on the same night, I think one was called Catstac."

"That's it and his brother had a strange sounding name, something like Milglim, we used to play hunt the turnip and he usually won."

"I'm sure he cheated," said Pullup. "He looked through his fingers when we were hiding it."

"Never mind, he hasn't cheated on anybody for a long, long time," Romanamor interrupted.

"Now we'd better get a move on and find some more."

They crept off into the night, silent now, because they did not know what was around the next corner. Naggan had hardly spoken a word since he was rescued, apart from to his mother that is, but this was not surprising really, as he had been brought up in isolation and was not used to mixing with other gnomes. Secretly though, he was rather enjoying the company and was planning in his own mind to try and persuade his mum and dad to move back to Grassroot.

Grattarg was back to his old self, laughing and joking all the time. Cramarc had to tell him to be quiet on a number of occasions.

Romanamor got very angry with him when he started hiding behind trees and making elf noises. Grattarg realised he was being silly and apologised at once, from then on he travelled in silence with the others.

The irony of Grattarg making elf noises was lost on the gnomes, who were unaware of just how quickly the real elves were moving.

Chapter 12

The Elves Arrive at the Village

The first two groups of elves, led by Snitchmire and Prodlife respectively, had met up on the outskirts of the village and were huddled together, planning the best way to search for the gnomes.

"We'd better spread out, we don't want to miss anything," said Snitchmire.

"We won't," hissed Prodlife. "We know every inch of this place; those stupid gnomes haven't got a chance."

The other elves cackled at the thought of what they were going to do to the gnomes when they caught them.

"It'll be far more fun if they don't go solid," laughed one.

"We can take them away and use them as slaves," agreed another.

"We have to catch them first." Snitchmire pointed out. "Did you manage to steal some rope, Squiggly?"

"Of course," came the reply. "I've got it here in my sack. I think there's enough to tie up at least 20 of the ugly ones."

"It must be very thin then," commented Snitchmire. "Are you sure it's strong enough?"

"I got it from one of those places where humans tie up big blocks of dead grass," said Squiggly. "It is definitely strong enough."

"Good," replied Snitchmire. "And now, my evil little friends, let's go and catch us some gnomes."

With that, the elves moved off into the village. More elves would be arriving soon, and one of them volunteered to stay behind to inform them as to what was going on.

What the elves encountered in the village surprised them slightly. The elves knew where all the gnomes were that had been brought to Humanland and they didn't expect to see them still in their original positions. Something's wrong here, thought Prodlife, as he looked across at the garden where the gnomes had rescued Naggan. Prodlife was trying to get it straight in his head, if these gnomes are being recovered, how come they are still here? Maybe the potion hadn't worked after all.

The recently rescued gnomes were aware of the elves watching them and kept very, very still. In the end the elves reached a conclusion that the gnomes hadn't yet found this garden and they slowly walked round it and disappeared into the night.

Checking more gardens, the elves soon realised that all the gnomes were still there and not suspecting any trickery on the part of the gnomes, came to the understanding that one way or another, the family who had come to save the solid gnomes had not been successful. But as we know, the mission was very successful and was continuing to be so. In fact, more and more gnomes were being saved.

Chapter 13

Finding the Workshop

Cramarc was very upset because they hadn't yet found Potstop, but Romanamor tried to be optimistic.

"He's bound to be somewhere in the village," he said.

"What if he's been taken to another village?" Asked Cramarc.

"I don't think so; the elves are far too lazy to travel any further than they have to," replied Romanamor.

"We will find him then, no matter how long it takes," said Cramarc, beginning to feel more positive.

The village wasn't a very large one and the gnomes had been very busy during the night. Unfortunately Potstop still had not been found and it seemed like they were approaching the end of the village. Dawn was breaking and in the half-light they could make out the fields and woodland beyond the houses. They had used the potion to rescue many, many gnomes and were now becoming concerned about how much they had left. They were unsure about how long they could safely leave between doses for themselves and there were only two flagons remaining, of which one was only about three-quarters full.

"We need to save enough so we can get back home safely," whispered Tromort.

"I agree," said Romanamor. "We can always come back with some more potion; we've done it once, we can do it again."

A far more immediate question was on Agninga's mind. "Where are we going to hide for the day? There doesn't seem to be anywhere round here."

"I think we'll make our way to the woods beyond the village," said Romanamor.

"We'd better go straight away, it's going to be light very soon."

They set off as fast as their weary legs would carry them and were only just clear of the houses when the sun came up over the horizon.

They hurried across the fields to the nearest area of woodland. Naggan was completely exhausted, he hadn't yet recovered from being solid and he collapsed under the nearest tree.

"I think we're going to have to go a bit deeper into the woods," said Romanamor. "Any humans going past could see us quite easily if we stay here."

Tromort picked up Naggan, laid him on the cart and began pushing it through the woods. The rest of the gnomes followed, with the children plodding behind. Gnomes weren't built for the kind of exercise these gnomes had been getting, and they were all ready for a good long sleep.

They hadn't gone far into the woods when they came across an old, wooden shack. Everything about the shack told the gnomes that it was uninhabited, but they still approached it very cautiously, as if someone or something, might still be there. Romanamor decided to go and have a quick peep through the window on his own, motioning to the others to stay out of sight. The window was a bit too high for him to see through, but he found a piece of sawn-off log nearby and dragged it over to the shack. Standing on the log, he could just see over the edge of the window frame. As he peered in, he could see that it appeared to be some kind of workshop, there were large tins of paint and some woodworking equipment on a table at the back of the shack.

"Humans come here," he mumbled to himself. "Maybe it's not a good place to hide." He returned to the others and told them what he had seen.

"I shouldn't think they actually live here; they probably only use it as a workshop," said Tromort.

"That's possible," mused Romanamor.

"I mean, if they were living here, why aren't they here now?" Questioned Tromort.

"I say we take a chance. After all, it's going to be far safer than just sleeping in the woods," said Cramarc.

"All right then, that's what we'll do," agreed Romanamor. "But we'll have to hide the cart here. We can take the potion with us in case it gets stolen."

There was no latch on the door, so it was easily opened, but it creaked noisily and the gnomes anxiously kept looking round, in case the creaking disturbed some unknown enemy in the woods. Inside it was fairly dark, but they could still see all the things that Romanamor had described to them. On closer inspection, the paint was mainly red, in fact the same shade of red that the kidnapped gnomes were painted. Under the table were all sorts of gnome-sized things, such as fishing rods, wheelbarrows, spades, forks and various other garden implements.

The family soon came to the conclusion that they had stumbled across the very place where kidnapped gnomes were transformed into human ornaments. In the corner of the shed was a large blanket, it was old and dusty, but the gnomes thought it would be safer to hide under it than just sleep on the floor, where any humans coming in would see them straight away. Romanamor lifted the blanket up very gingerly; you never know what sort of creature might find it a good resting place.

There wasn't anything dangerous under the blanket, but in the corner sat a rather sad-looking gnome. He was covered in dust and cobwebs, but even through them he was instantly recognisable to Romanamor and Cramarc.

"Potstop!" They exclaimed simultaneously.

Pullup and Tippit rushed over to the corner of the shed to have a look under the blanket.

"It is, it is!" Shouted Pullup, overjoyed at seeing his brother again.

Tippit acted calmer but was nevertheless just as excited. Cramarc bent over and gently picked up her youngest son and whilst she cradled him in her arms, Romanamor poured a small amount of potion onto his lips.

After a while, Potstop's eyes flickered open. His last memory was of being picked up and carried into the shack by some strange looking giant and the panic of those last few moments before he was hidden under the blanket, remained with him.

"Evael em enola! Tup em nwod! He shouted.

"It's all right Potstop, it's us, your mum and dad," said Cramarc.

"On s'ti ton s'ti a tnaig."

"It's not a giant, it's really us," said Romanamor. "We've been looking for you everywhere."

Cramarc gently rocked Potstop back and forth trying to get his spiral brain and thus his speech in the right direction. Pullup and Tippit looked on, concerned about why it was taking so long for their brother to recognise them.

"Krad, krad, please don't put me back in the dark," pleaded Potstop.

Cramarc's rocking motion seemed to be having some effect. It took a long time for the magic potion to circulate, but eventually it reached his spiral brain and he began to think more clearly. He looked around him until his eyes rested on Pullup and Tippit.

"Is it really you?" He asked. "Or am I just dreaming?"

Tippit reached over and gave his nose a friendly tweak. "Can dreams do that?" He asked.

"It really is you," said Potstop excitedly. "I never thought I'd see you again."

Cramarc put Potstop gently down onto his feet. He wanted to move about freely straight away, but it was all he could do to put one leg in front of the other.

"Don't worry, the stiffness wears off after a while," explained Tippit.

"How come you know so much?" Enquired Potstop.

"We've rescued lots of gnomes before we found you," said Cramarc.

Romanamor gave Potstop a brief outline about how they got there and what it was they used to make the solid gnomes come back to life.

"You must love me very much to have gone to all that trouble," said Potstop, tearfully.

"When you were kidnapped, it was as if a great big empty hole had come into our lives," said Cramarc.

"With that in mind, we had no choice but to make every effort to try and get you back," explained Romanamor.

"We are only travelling at night. We're going to stay here for the day and I'm afraid that means going back under the blanket," apologised Cramarc.

"Oh I don't mind if you're there," said Potstop, confidently. "I haven't heard the giant for ages, I think he must have gone away."

"Well I hope you're right, now let's get under the blanket and get some sleep," yawned Tromort.

There was just about enough room for everyone, with the two male gnomes sleeping on the outside so that the others would feel protected. Unfortunately, there was nothing they could do about the one thing that would give them away, should anyone come. Their snoring was amplified in the shack and anyone or anything walking past would be bound to hear them.

No human came near that day, but something far worse was lurking on the edge of the woods.

Chapter 14

Captured by Elves

Two elf spies had been searching gardens on this side of the village and at dawn had decided that the woods were a good place to hide for the day. They were familiar with these woods and knew where the shack was located, for they had brought kidnapped gnomes up here many times in the past.

"Let's go and see if the human's still there," said one of the elves.

"We're going to need him when we finally catch up with the gnomes."

"Good idea," said the other one. "Maybe we'll come across some gnomes in the woods."

"Yeah, and we can take the credit for finding them," sniggered the first one.

"Come on."

The elves set off through the woods toward the shack. It was broad daylight now and they moved swiftly from tree to tree in case there were humans around. But there were no humans and they were soon in sight of the shack. They slowed down at this point and crept in their sneaky, elf-like fashion towards it. All seemed quiet until they got really close; they stopped and listened.

"Can you hear snoring?" Asked the first elf.

"I'm sure I can," whispered the other one. "Only gnomes snore like that."

"They must be inside; these gnomes are more stupid than we thought."

"Let's have a closer look."

The elves inched slowly towards the shack, then they crept around to the front and slowly opened the door.

"They're definitely inside," said the first one.

"They're trapped. Let's go in," said the second, an evil grin spreading over his pointed face. Even through the old blanket the elves could still pick up the scent of the gnomes. They didn't want to risk the gnomes waking up and escaping, so they didn't bother lifting up the blanket, they didn't need to confirm the presence of the gnomes, because the snoring and the strong scent had already given away the hiding place.

The elves grinned at each other, we are going to make ourselves very popular with Snitchmire and Prodlife, they thought to themselves. They were still grinning when they emerged from the shack and made their way back through the woods. They would spend all day informing as many elves as they could find of the whereabouts of the gnomes.

Using their knowledge of the usual hiding places, they made contact with 20 or so elves and told them to be in the woods, near the shack by nightfall.

They espied Prodlife fast asleep, in the large yew tree, next to the churchyard. He didn't like being woken up and spat and cursed at the two elves who had interrupted his beauty sleep. When he learned of the reason for them waking him however, his attitude changed.

"You have done well you nosy, little creeps. I will make sure that you are rewarded."

"Thank you, thank you, master," grovelled the spies. "We will leave you to your rest now and go and find some others."

Prodlife was asleep again as soon as the two elves had gone.

"Did you hear that? We're going to be rewarded," snickered one spy.

"If he remembers," said the other one as they walked off to try and alert some more elves.

Eventually they decided that enough elves had been informed and made their way back to the woods.

Meanwhile, the gnomes slept blissfully on, completely unaware of the danger that would be lurking outside, when they awoke.

All the elves that had been told where the gnomes were located, began making their way through the village, in the direction of the woods.

Some of the elves had told others and by late afternoon over 40 elves had arrived in the woods and were hiding, either in trees or behind bushes near to the shack. They hadn't been able to locate Snitchmire, but Prodlife was there with his right-hand man, Squiggly.

"Still got the rope, have you?" Asked Prodlife.

"Of course master, it's right here in my sack," replied Squiggly. "We're going to tie these gnomes up good and proper so they'll never get out."

"I think we've got enough elves here now, we might as well get on with it," hissed Prodlife.

"Yes, let's do it now. I don't want to wait any longer," said Squiggly, rubbing his pointed, little hands together.

"I'll go in first, just to make sure there aren't too many of them and you two," said Prodlife, pointing at the elf spies who had found the gnomes. "You two, have a look around and see if you can find this magic potion that makes the gnomes braver. If you find it, we'll take it with us."

The two spies beamed with self-importance; it wasn't often that any elves were singled out for special duties.

Inside the shack the gnomes were waking up. Tromort was the first to pull back the blanket and check that everything was all right. He looked around and nodded to the others. "Seems quiet enough," he whispered.

"Too quiet if you ask me," said Romanamor. "Why aren't the birds singing? There's definitely something that isn't quite right."

Tromort crept over to the door and peered out.

"Everything looks normal, but you are right about the silence."

All of a sudden, the silence was broken by the dreaded sound of elfin laughter. As Tromort watched, Prodlife walked out into the clearing in front of the shack.

"Ah! A real, live gnome at last," he sneered. "We've been searching everywhere for you."

Tromort stood transfixed in the doorway, he wanted to run, but his legs couldn't move. As he watched, other elves began appearing from the bushes behind Prodlife. The potion had stopped him going solid at the sight of all these elves, but it did not stop him from being scared.

He panicked and slammed the door shut, as if not being able to see them would make them go away. The other gnomes were all wide awake by this time and had climbed out from behind the blanket.

"What's going on," asked Agninga. "You don't normally slam doors."

"We're, we're, we're surrounded yb sevle," stammered Tromort, struggling to stop his speech from going completely backwards.

"How many?" Asked Romanamor.

"Lots and lots of them," said Tromort. "And I don't think they've come for a tea party."

"No, we haven't," came a sneering voice from the other side of the door. We've come for a tie-up party."

The elves behind Prodlife all cackled at the joke and Prodlife and Squiggly between them yanked open the door.

"Nice of you gnomes to make your own way here," said Prodlife. "It saves us the trouble of carrying you."

"Come on, let's tie them up," hissed Squiggly, getting the rope out of his sack.

Prodlife gestured to the other elves to follow them into the shack.

This is going to be easy, he thought.

But it wasn't easy at all. The gnomes, although not normally aggressive, were very strong and these particular gnomes, fired up as they were with large doses of the magic potion, were proving quite a handful for the elves to overcome. Romanamor and Tromort put up a heroic fight.

They were picking up the elves and throwing them outside, but the elves, who were enjoying every minute of this, were coming back in as quickly as they went out.

The gnomes were eventually overwhelmed by the sheer number of elves, and Squiggly managed to tie them up, one by one. The children first, then Agninga and Cramarc and finally Romanamor and Tromort were bound hand and foot. They were made to sit down along one wall of the shack. Prodlife beamed in triumph, for he knew that back home in Elfland, he, and not Snitchmire, would become the number one son.

Worse was yet to come for the poor gnomes. The two elf spies had found the flagons of potion and were carrying them out of the shack.

"We know this stuff doesn't work, but were taking it anyway," said Prodlife.

"How do you know it doesn't work?" Asked Romanamor.

"Because if it was any good, at least some of the gnomes would have been rescued by now, but all the ones we've seen are still in the gardens," answered Prodlife.

"Don't be too confident," said Romanamor. "You could be in for quite a few surprises."

"You're the ones who were taken by surprise," sneered Prodlife.

"No one ever surprises us."

"You'll see," said Tromort. "You nasty little creatures will get your come-uppance."

"Not from you we won't," laughed Prodlife, jabbing at Tromort with his pointed stick.

Cramarc, Agninga and the children were so shocked and scared by what had just happened, they were totally speechless.

"We'll leave you in peace now," said Prodlife. "It won't be long before you go nice and solid, ready for a coat of that beautiful red paint."

The gnomes just stared back in silence.

"Bye-bye gnomes, it was nice to have met you," said Prodlife, sarcastically. And with that, the elves left the shack.

As soon as the elves had gone, Romanamor began trying to free himself. He strained against the knots around his wrists and ankles, then he shook his arms and legs trying to loosen the knots. He tried everything he could think of to break himself free, but it was no use. Squiggly had tied the knots too tightly and there was no way of escape. The others sat watching Romanamor struggle, for if he couldn't free himself, what chance would they have?

Finally Romanamor gave up. He was red in the face and beads of sweat were beginning to appear on his forehead.

"It's no use, we'll never get out of here," he said despondently.

"Ton dilos niaga os noos," cried Naggan.

"Maybe one of the gnomes we've rescued will come and save us," said Agninga, trying to be reassuring.

"I'd like to think so, but the trouble is, we've told all the rescued gnomes to head back towards home," Romanamor sighed.

"On noitop ew og dilos," stammered Grattarg, just about managing to get the words out.

"How long will it be before the potion that we've taken wears off?" Asked Cramarc.

"Nobody knows," answered Romanamor. "Nobody knows," he tapered off, sadly.

The elves were very cocky and confident when they walked back towards the village. It was dark now and the elves didn't have to skulk through the back gardens like they normally did. They became so bold, that they were almost seen by the humans a couple of times, but such was the buoyancy of their mood, that they didn't care.

Once they got into the centre of the village however, Prodlife told them to keep a little more hidden. Whilst they were travelling, the elves were passing around the flagons of potion. Some of the elves didn't want to pass it on and much squabbling ensued. Prodlife got quite angry with them and jabbed a few with his pointed stick.

"Keep it quiet," he hissed. "We're getting near the building where all the humans come at night."

The elves were indeed, approaching the public house. To avoid it, they went into the churchyard on the opposite side of the road, the very place where the gnomes had hidden on the previous night. From their position in the churchyard, the elves had a good view of the garden and what they saw, or rather what they didn't see, left them totally dumbfounded. The gnomes in the pub garden had all gone! The barrows, garden implements and fishing rods were piled in a heap in the corner but there was absolutely no sign of any gnomes.

"What's going on?" Asked Prodlife, of no one in particular. "They were all here last night and now they're not."

"Maybe one of the other humans has stolen them," suggested Squiggly.

"Then why would they leave the fishing rods and things behind?" Questioned Prodlife.

"Too much to carry?" Said Squiggly, hopefully.

"Nonsense!" Exclaimed Prodlife. "I think that these gnomes have made their own way out of here."

Prodlife had to think quickly, he designated some of the elves to go round to the other gardens and see if the gnomes were still there.

The elves rushed off to do as they were told, for they knew that Prodlife was in a very bad mood indeed. Searching the other gardens didn't take long and one by one the elves returned. They all had the same bad news, apart from the plastic replicas made by humans, there were no gnomes to be seen anywhere.

Prodlife started to panic, how could he tell Snitchmire, or the Duke and Duchess, that all the gnomes had disappeared?

"We must find them and get them back," he said. "They can't have been gone for long."

"Surely they must be headed for home," suggested Squiggly. "If we can get back to the tunnel before they do, we can stop them going through."

"Just what I was thinking," snapped Prodlife, angry at being outthought by one of his minions.

"Come on you revolting lot, let's get back there as soon as possible."

So this particular gang of elves began making their way towards the tunnel using every short-cut they knew, so as to get there as quickly as they could.

Chapter 15

Pingnip Effects a Rescue

The reason that Snitchmire had disappeared from the scene, was that he and some of the other elves had stolen some of the fiery liquid that the humans drink and were living it up in a disused barn on the other side of the village.

The rescued gnomes however, had not done as the elves had anticipated. After much debating, they had decided to stay in Humanland until all the gnomes, including their rescuers, could get back to Gnomeland safely. There were some who wanted to get back home as soon as possible, but the majority felt it was their duty to help as many gnomes as they could. They split up into small groups, so they would be less likely to be detected, then they went off in search of others.

One particular gnome was feeling bolder and more adventurous than the other gnomes; his name was Pingnip. He decided to go it alone, because the rest of the group that were with him was very nervous about venturing too far from the other groups. Despite the other gnomes trying to stop him, Pingnip was determined to cover as much ground as he could before daybreak. Why was he so much braver than the others? Probably because one of the rescuers had given him far more potion than was needed, just to bring him round.

Anyway, off he went as fast as his little gnome legs would carry him. He still ached after being solid for so long, but the overdose of potion helped him to ignore the pain. He searched all of the garden sheds and other places where gnomes may have hidden themselves.

He came across the old barn where Snitchmire's gang of elves were still partying. He froze when he heard the elfin laughter and it took every ounce of his willpower to get himself moving again. He got as far away from the old barn as he possibly could, because if they caught him, a solitary gnome would be a great source of wicked amusement, to a bunch of drunken elves.

He carried on searching, occasionally meeting other groups of recovering gnomes; he didn't stop to talk because he was determined to find the ones who had rescued him. By sunrise he had searched nearly all the village and was completely exhausted. The effects of the extra potion were beginning to wear off and he needed to find somewhere safe to hide. He was on the edge of the village by now and from where he stood, he could see a small expanse of woodland on the other side of some fields. Pingnip decided that this would be a good place to rest and he used his last reserves of energy getting there. He didn't feel safe on the edge of the woods and decided to venture further in.

Apart from the birdsong, it was very peaceful in the woods and as he walked, he couldn't help thinking of the life that he used to lead back in Gnomeland. His memory had been dulled over the years, but it was slowly coming back. He remembered his mother and father, also his three brothers and wondered if any of them had been kidnapped. He became very sad at the thought of not seeing them again.

By now he had reached the middle of the woods and he began to realise that there was another sound there, apart from the birdsong. It was a kind of very faint snoring sound, and as he walked, the sound got louder. He knew somewhere deep in the back of his mind what it was. It related somehow to the time before he became solid. All of a sudden, it came back to him, it was the sound of snoring gnomes. He stopped and listened, then he began walking in the direction that he thought the sound was coming from. It wasn't long before he had pinpointed the exact source of the snoring. He had found the shack and the noise was definitely coming from inside. He moved cautiously towards it and pulled open the door and there, still bound hand and foot, were the gnomes who had been his rescuers.

Except for one of the female gnomes, they were all fast asleep.

"Hello, my names Pingnip, how on earth did you manage to get tied up in here?"

"Thank goodness, someone's found us," said a very relieved Cramarc.

"The elves found us hiding here and thought that if they tied us up, we would go solid and be stuck here forever."

Cramarc and Pingnip awoke the other gnomes. There were mixed looks of surprise and relief on all of their faces.

"How did you find us?" Asked Tromort. "We thought we'd had it."

"Luck," answered Pingnip. "I was looking for somewhere to hide and heard your snoring."

Grattarg looked across at Pingnip, a glimmer of recognition in his eyes.

"I remember you, you're Pingnip aren't you?"

"That's right, I think I remember you as well. Didn't we used to play together back in Stonemarble?"

"Yes, I'm Grattarg, your dad worked with mine in the apple orchard."

"Your memory is much better than mine, I just hope I can still recall how to untie knots," said Pingnip.

"Mine don't seem too tight," said Tromort. "Try and untie me first."

Pingnip knelt down and began picking at the knots. His stubby, gnome fingers made it very difficult to do anything fiddly, but he was very determined and persevered until they finally came undone.

"Thank you," Said Tromort, shaking his hands, to try and get the circulation back.

"Thank you, thank you." He repeated, not really knowing what else to say.

“You saved me, and now I'm saving you,” explained Pingnip, already moving on to try and untie Cramarc.

“I'll give you a hand, I seem to be able to move my fingers now,” said Tromort.

Between them, they soon had all of the gnomes untied. Romanamor, not normally given to showing signs of emotion, clasped Pingnip firmly by the shoulders, in a sort of half-embrace.

“Thanks Pingnip,” he said. “We honestly thought that no one would ever find us up here.”

Pingnip became rather embarrassed and was a bit overcome by all the gratitude he was receiving.

“As I just said, I am only repaying the favour of you rescuing me.”

“Nevertheless, it was a brave act of yours, coming into these woods all by yourself,” said Romanamor. “And now I suggest we make some plans to get back home.”

“I think we should avoid the village altogether,” said Tromort.

“Without any potion, we can't take a chance of being scared by anyone.”

“I think that we should just hide in the woods until nighttime. I don't want to stay in this shack any longer in case the human comes,” said Agninga.

They all agreed that it would be far safer hiding in the woods and Romanamor led the gnomes out of the shack.

Grattarg, Naggan, Pingnip and Potstop were still covered in bright red paint.

"I think we ought to try and get some of that horrible red stuff cleaned off," said Cramarc. "It's going to be very hard to hide in the woods when you're so brightly coloured."

It was only the clothing that had been painted and the four gnomes took off their jackets, trousers and hats so that they could be cleaned. The adult gnomes set about trying to get the paint off the clothes. They tried scratching it off, beating it off, rubbing it with leaves, rubbing it with tree bark, in fact they tried every method that they could think of, but nothing would remove the red paint.

"I'm afraid that you're stuck with being this colour until we can get you some new clothes," sighed Cramarc.

Tromort had an idea. "If we can just make the clothes very dirty, they won't be so visible."

Everyone agreed that this would have to do for the time being. They dug down under the leaves, where they knew that the soil would be dark and damp, because they used the same kind of soil on their vegetable patches. They rubbed the clothes in the dark mud and eventually most of the red had been covered.

"That's better." Said Romanamor.

"We can't put these on, they're all wet," moaned Naggan.

"We'll have to spread them out for the day to dry," said Cramarc. "It's going to be a nice sunny day, so you won't be too cold without them."

Naggan had an idea; he motioned to Potstop to follow him. They went back to the shack and a short while later, returned with the old blanket.

"Just in case it gets cold," explained Naggan.

The gnomes found a place to rest for the day and settled down. They had not had anything to eat for quite a long time and were very hungry. Tromort had trouble sleeping that day because his rumbling tummy kept him awake.

I must find food soon, he thought to himself. When he did sleep, he dreamed of his vegetable plot back in Gnomeland, or of Agninga cooking vegetables on the open stove.

The others, who didn't have quite such large appetites as Tromort, slept soundly.

Chapter 16

The Builders Find the Village

The builders who had followed the elves through the tunnel had finally come across the village. It was more by luck than anything else, as the builders had over the years, lost the sixth sense of direction that ordinary gnomes possess. They didn't really need it in their trade because the only travelling they did was to the quarry and back. It was dawn now and they were looking for somewhere to hide, well away from the village.

"How about down there?" Said Toocoot, pointing to a ruined building, at the bottom of an overgrown field.

"That'll do us," said Roccor. "It looks like it hasn't been used for years."

Roccor was right about that. It hadn't been used for years, by humans that is, but someone or something was using it at this very minute. As the builders approached, they could hear a faint, snoring sound. Toocoot went on ahead and peered through the window. What he saw took him completely by surprise, for there, in the building were a dozen or so young gnomes, all fast asleep.

"Come and look," he said to the other builders.

"They must be gnomes that have already been rescued," said Roccor.

"Shall we wake them up?"

"No, they look so peaceful, it wouldn't be fair," said Granarg. "We'll just try and find some room for ourselves, without disturbing them."

The builders managed to squeeze into the building and find somewhere to lie down. It was a bit like a gnome version of sardines, the game that humans play, where they try and fit as many people, into a small space, as they can. They were all soon fast asleep, happy to have found somewhere safe and also happy that they had at last found the village.

Unbeknown to them, they had only just taken cover in time. Prodlife and his gang of elves had worked their way across the village during the night and were passing the top of the overgrown field at the same time as the gnomes were settling down. The elves were in a hurry and didn't even bother to send out the spies that they normally would have done. Prodlife's main aim was to get back to the tunnel as quickly as possible.

Elsewhere in the village, Snitchmire and the drunken revellers with him, were finally sobering up. It was now broad daylight and they decided to stay where they were so that they could sleep off the effects of the previous night's drink. Meanwhile, more and more elves had been making their way through the tunnel and were now camped near the entrance. Prodlife and his group of elves would be joining them by the end of the day. Eventually Snitchmire and his followers would also be heading for the tunnel, thereby making it impossible for the gnomes to get back home.

Chapter 17

Frogorf Enters the Tunnel

The elves were very confident in their ability to stop the gnomes, but what they didn't know was that Frogorf and 30 or so builders, were heading through Gnomeland towards the mountains. At the same time as Prodlife reached the tunnel at the Humanland end, Frogorf and the builders were entering the tunnel at the Gnomeland end.

Frogorf was in high spirits. To be back with his fellow gnomes again after all those years in the wilderness had given him a new lease of life. As they got deeper into the tunnel, they travelled as quietly as they could because they didn't know what would be awaiting them around the next bend. Elves have a nasty habit of jumping out on unsuspecting gnomes and they didn't want to give them advance warning of their approach.

As it turned out, the builders had no cause to worry as all of the elves were camped at the other end of the tunnel and none of them had ventured into it. The builders did not find negotiating the tunnel easy, there were many twists and turns and in some places, it became so narrow that they had to squeeze through, one gnome at a time. Luckily the carts that they had brought with them were long, narrow ones otherwise there would have been no way of getting them through. It took them even longer than it had taken Romanamor and the family to reach the other end and despite their great stamina, the builders were on the point of collapse when they finally reached it. The tunnel became much wider approaching the exit and there was a large cave on one side where the builders decided to stop and rest for a while. Just a couple of hours' sleep was enough to refresh them and they were soon awake, making plans for their next move.

A builder called Raggar seemed to be the one making all the decisions, it wasn't that he was a leader, or anything like that, it's just that he was the eldest and gnomes always have great respect for their elders.

"Before we all go blundering into the unknown," he said. "We need to know a little bit about what's out there, I think we should send a couple of volunteers to scout around and see if it's safe."

Two of the younger builders said that they would go and make sure the surrounding area was clear of elves. This was acceptable to the others and they were both given a large dose of potion each, just in case anything was out there. The builders knew absolutely nothing about Humanland, and any amount of surprises could be awaiting them. The two young gnomes, whose names were Emertreme and Dortrod, didn't have to venture far into Humanland to see evidence that elves were present.

From where they stood, a few dozen yards from the tunnel exit, they could see plumes of smoke coming from every clump of bushes.

"Do you think this means?" Asked Emertreme.

"Almost certainly," replied Dortrod.

They both knew instinctively what the other was thinking.

"They're guarding the tunnel from this side now," whispered Emertreme, still not daring to mention the name.

"Let's try and get a bit closer," said Dortrod. "If we stay upwind, they won't be able to pick up our scent."

They could see which way the wind was blowing by watching the plumes of smoke, and they had to walk a long way before they decided that it was safe to circle round behind the bushes.

"Should be all right now," said Dortrod, quietly.

"Just as long as the wind doesn't change direction," Emertreme replied.

Luckily the wind stayed where it was and the gnomes were able to get close enough to see what was going on. They hid behind a large rock that had fallen down from the mountain and from this position, they could make out the thin figures of the elves, around the campfires.

"How many do you think there are?" Whispered Dortrod.

"Let's see, um, if there are nine fires and six or seven elves around each one that's, um, an awful lot of elves," said Emertreme.

Gnomes weren't known for their ability to do mathematics, but they could go and tell the others how many fires there were and how many elves were camped around each one. The older gnomes might even be able to work out how many there were altogether.

"Come on, let's go back and report to the others," said Dortrod.

They made their way back to the tunnel and then into the cave where the others were sat waiting. They explained exactly what they had seen to the gnomes in the cave. Raggar thought carefully before he spoke. He was trying to calculate how many elves there were and it took him a lot of time and effort before he reached a conclusion.

Finally, he spoke.

"By my workings out, there must be between 60 and 70 elves out there and goodness knows how many in the surrounding area. I don't think we should risk a confrontation with them unless it becomes absolutely necessary."

The other builders nodded in agreement.

He went on.

"Now if we wait until it gets dark, do you think that you two," he looked across at Emertreme and Dortrod.

"Do you think that you two would be able to sneak past the elves' camps and find out what's happening beyond them?"

"We can try," said Emertreme. "As long as we're well dosed up with potion, I'm sure we'll be all right."

"Brave lads!" Said Raggar. "We'll be waiting just inside the tunnel entrance, so if you get any trouble with the elves, shout and we'll come and help you."

The young builders were quite proud to be singled out for special duties, but they had to ensure that they didn't become over-confident. One slip up and they could be in real danger. The builders had brought with them large quantities of food and drink and they decided that now would be as good a time as any to have a meal.

Frogorf was feeling quite at home now with the builders, but he still felt that he wanted to do more to help. "I'd like to go with Dortrod and Emertreme," he said.

"I could be very useful if they get into any trouble."

"Very well," agreed Raggar. "But remember, the more of you go, the more careful you have to be not to be seen."

"Don't worry, we'll give the elves' camps a very wide berth indeed!" Said Frogorf, emphatically.

So it was agreed that Frogorf should accompany the two young builders into Humanland. It was a long time before nightfall, so the builders settled down for another rest, not knowing what might happen in the next 24 hours.

Chapter 18

Elves Return to Guard the Tunnel

Prodlife and his Elfin gang were now well on their way to joining the elves camped around the tunnel. They knew all the best routes they could take without being seen, and when they were away from the village weren't bothered about travelling during the day.

Snitchmire and the elves with him meanwhile, were coming round after their drunken binge. They all had very bad headaches and were not in a very good mood at all. Snitchmire, who had probably drunk the most, had a vile temper at the moment and was shouting at the other elves to find out what was going on. He ordered his best spies to go round the village and report back to him as quickly as they could. The elf spies went out and using all of their elf cunning, spread out and investigated what had been going on whilst they were otherwise engaged. The news they brought back to Snitchmire was not good. No matter where they looked, there weren't any gnomes in the entire village. The only ones to be seen were the copies that the humans made. As you can imagine this put Snitchmire in a worse mood than he had been in before.

"You lot are useless!" He screamed at the other elves. "How could you possibly let all these gnomes escape?"

The elves were far too scared of Snitchmire to ever argue with him, but they all knew that he was as much to blame as they were.

After he had calmed down a bit, Snitchmire began to think more clearly about what might have happened.

"They must be headed back to Gnomeland," he said. "We need to get to the tunnel entrance right away and stop them going through."

"But Snitchmire, we can't all leave at once, we're bound to be seen," said one of the elves.

"I know that, you stupid elf," hissed Snitchmire. "We'll have to leave in small groups, say five or six in each one and make sure that you keep clear of humans."

The elves organised themselves into small groups, but not without a lot of argument about who was going to be with who. Snitchmire and his two best spies waited until the other elves had gone before they made their move. Very soon all of the elves would be camped near the tunnel entrance, positive in their own minds, that no gnomes were ever going to get past them.

Chapter 19

Romanamor and Family Meet Roccor and Toocoot

On the other side of the village, Romanamor was just waking up. It was still daylight and it certainly wasn't time to make a move yet. Tromort was also awake, in fact, his rumbling stomach had kept him awake for most of the day.

"We must find some food soon," he grumbled. "I don't think that I'll have the energy to walk far without it."

"I'm hungry too, Tromort, but don't worry, we'll make finding food a priority as soon as it gets dark," consoled Romanamor.

"I was hoping you'd say that. All I can think of at the moment is fields full of cabbages."

They sat in silence for a while, gazing at their respective families and thinking that they must be hungry too.

"We've come a long way since we left Gnomeland," said Romanamor.

"And I'm beginning to wonder if we'll ever get back."

"Courage my friend," said Tromort. "With the help of the gnomes who have stayed behind, we have a very good chance of getting home."

"Don't forget that the elves are going to do everything in their power to stop us," said Romanamor, being his usual, realistic self.

"Ah yes, the elves," sighed Tromort. "Well I know what I'd like to do with their little pointed sticks."

Romanamor laughed at this. "I dream of the day when we'll be rid of the elves forever."

"So do I," agreed Tromort. "So do I."

Cramarc, Agninga and the rest of the gnomes were waking up now and they were all moaning about being hungry.

"We're going to search for food as soon as it gets dark," promised Romanamor.

Time passed very slowly for the gnomes as they waited for nightfall. Pullup and Tippit spent the time wondering around in the woods searching for something to eat but there was nothing edible growing anywhere.

There weren't even any wild strawberries or mushrooms, which in some woods were plentiful.

After what seemed like an eternity, the sun finally began to sink below the horizon and the dusky gloom of twilight descended on Humanland.

"Ready?" Asked Romanamor. "If we're very cautious, I think we can make a move now."

The younger gnomes were excited at the prospect of heading homeward and were laughing and joking about what they were going to do if they got back home.

"Don't forget, caution also includes being silent," said Cramarc.

"Sorry Mum," apologised Potstop. "From now on we shall be so quiet that you won't even know that we're here."

"Let's go then," said Romanamor, leading the way across the fields towards the village.

The gnomes had been resting for a long while and Romanamor was fairly confident that they could be well on the way to the tunnel entrance before daybreak.

In the tumble-down cottage, on the other side of the village, Granarg, Toocoot, Roccor and the rest of the builders were awake, as were the rescued gnomes who were crammed in with them. The rescued gnomes had explained to the builders how they came to be there and how they had been revived by the potion given to them by Romanamor and his family. They knew that the family had carried on through the village, but did not know where they were now. They were also very aware that there were elves in the vicinity because they had heard them going past.

The builders were very pleased to hear of the success that Romanamor and the family had been having. They decided that they should send out a search party to try and locate them.

"We'd better not all go, just a few of us would find it easier to avoid detection," said Granarg.

"So who goes and who stays?" Asked one of the builders.

"Well, I'd like to go," said Roccor. "And if I take Toocoot and four others with me, I think we should be able to cope."

Granarg readily agreed to Roccor's suggestion, in fact he was quite relieved by that fact that his name hadn't been mentioned. Being a great deal older and slower than the others, he thought that if he were to go, he would only hold the others back.

"If you come across anything untoward, let us know straight away."

"Don't worry Granarg, we will," said Roccor. "And we'll definitely be back before daylight."

"Good luck," said Granarg, as the six gnomes left the safety of the cottage.

"We'll bring back some food if we find any," shouted Toocoot, as he went out through the broken-down doorway.

It was very hard for them to stay hidden; they weren't used to lots of bright lights and the humans seemed to have lights everywhere. There were streetlights, house lights, even garden lights, and it was difficult for them to stay in the dark areas.

Nevertheless, they managed to negotiate their way through the village in comparative safety.

Romanamor, Cramarc and the gnomes with them had made it to the outskirts of the village and were picking their way slowly through it, using as much cover as they could. In one of the gardens, in a small plot hidden behind a hedge, was an area where a human had been growing various types of vegetables.

"Runner beans, my favourite," whispered Tromort. "Come on, let's get stuck in."

The gnomes did as Tromort suggested and ate as much as they could in the space of time that Romanamor had allotted for a break. After eating, they moved on and now they were thinking much more clearly as they were no longer worried about being hungry.

Within half an hour, they came to the road. Crossing this would be one of the most dangerous parts of their journey, for not only was it brightly lit, they had to avoid the large metal carts on wheels that came hurtling down it. They found a spot, away from the houses, so they wouldn't be seen and when they couldn't hear the roaring noise of the cars, they ran across as fast as they could to the safety of some trees on the other side. Tromort was pushing the cart, which made a loud rattling noise as he hurried with it over the tarmac. They had to stop for a moment to get their breath back and then they continued on their way using the trees as cover. Suddenly they stopped again, stopped and listened; there was the sound of heavy footsteps coming from the other side of the trees. The footsteps seemed to be coming in their direction and Romanamor motioned to the others to find somewhere to hide. They only just hid themselves in time, for the footsteps, or rather the owners of the footsteps became visible, well as visible as anything could be at night.

Peering round the tree at the shadowy figures coming their way, Romanamor could make out some very familiar shapes. The more he looked, the more familiar the shapes became, until finally there was no doubt what they were.

"They are definitely gnomes." He whispered to Cramarc, who was hiding behind the same tree as him.

"What are they doing here?" Asked Cramarc.

"Probably searching for us," answered Romanamor. "I'm going to ask them."

With that, he stepped out from behind the tree.

"Hello, I'm Romanamor, who might you be?"

"Nice to meet you again, remember us?" Asked Roccor.

"Of course, it's Roccor and Toocoot isn't it? You helped us get away from Gnomeland."

"Where are the rest of you?" Wondered Roccor.

"Are we relieved to see you!" Said another voice and Tromort stepped out of hiding.

The rest of the hiding gnomes felt brave enough to show themselves now and they were all very pleased to see the builders. Cramarc was quite overcome by the moment and gave Roccor a big hug. Gnomes, as you probably realise by now, are not known for showing emotion and Roccor was totally overcome by Cramarc's reaction.

"It's good to see you as well," he stammered. "How are you coping?"

"Not very well I'm afraid," said Romanamor. "We've been tied up by the elves and if it wasn't for Pingnip here, we would still be there."

He went on to explain what had happened and how Pingnip had come to their rescue. "Unfortunately, the elves have stolen our potion and we're worried about going solid if we should meet any danger."

"We have more than enough potion back at our hiding place," comforted Roccor.

"Are you the only builders who came through the tunnel?" Asked Tromort.

"No, there are 18 of us altogether, plus about a dozen young gnomes, who were already hiding in the old cottage that we chose as a place to stop," explained Toocoot.

"Is it far away?" Asked Cramarc.

"Not too far, but we'll be safer walking round the outskirts of the village, it should still only take a couple of hours," said Toocoot.

"I think we had better be making a move now," said Roccor. "We want to get back before daylight."

They set off at a fairly fast pace, not wanting to be out in the open when dawn came.

"Have you seen any elves in the village?" Asked Romanamor.

"Much to our surprise, we haven't seen any at all," answered one of the builders.

"We haven't seen any either, do you think something's scared them off?" Said Tromort.

"I doubt it, I should think that they've probably realised by now that all the gnomes have been brought back to life and of course, if we all go back to Gnomeland, the humans won't want to risk trading with them anymore," replied Roccor.

"They're bound to be waiting for us somewhere," said Romanamor.

"Almost certainly," agreed Roccor. "I should think the most likely place would be near the entrance to the caves."

"So how are we going to get past them?" Asked Agninga, sounding very worried.

"Maybe we'll have to fight our way through," Said Toocoot.

"'I hope you've got enough potion then," said Tromort. "It would be very hard to fight if we went solid."

It took them longer than they had estimated to get back to where Granarg and the others were waiting. They were almost seen by some humans when someone had switched on a patio light just as they were walking past. They moved as quickly as they could into the deep shadows of a hedge at the back of the garden, getting there at the same time as two humans came out of the house and headed for the table and chairs which were situated near the light. Very carefully and quietly they made their way along the hedge until they found a gap that was big enough for them to squeeze through.

"That was a close thing," whispered Tromort.

The others nodded in silent agreement. They continued the journey in silence, after the shock that they'd just had, they thought it better not to talk at all.

The rest of the journey passed without any more scary moments and they arrived safely at the tumble-down cottage.

Roccor popped his head round the doorway.

"We're back," he called. "And look who we've brought with us."

Granarg peered cautiously out of the doorway.

"Well crumble my granite!" He exclaimed. "You seem to have found all of them."

"It was half and half really," explained Roccor. "Half we found them, and half they found us."

"Well never mind who found who. I'm just pleased you got back here safely."

"Have you used much potion since we've been gone?" Asked Roccor.

"We haven't needed to use any at all, things have been very quiet and all the young gnomes seem to have recovered from their ordeal," said Granarg.

"That's good," said Roccor. "Because I think that we're going to need as much as possible to get us safely back home."

"If you all feel up to it," said Granarg, "I think we should make a move now. We could be well clear of the village before the humans start waking up."

"I'm fine," said Romanamor. "What about the rest of you?"

"We'll survive," said Agninga. "The thought of returning home will keep us going."

So the gnomes left the sanctuary of the cottage, and with Romanamor and Tromort leading the way, set off for home.

"And what about elves?" Asked Granarg, as they walked along. "Have you seen any? Fortunately we haven't, how about you?" Said Roccor.

"We saw a few of the blighters walking past at the top of the field, but they seemed intent on getting somewhere and didn't stop to bother us," said Granarg.

"We've come to the conclusion that all of the elves are moving towards the tunnel, so they can try and stop us getting back through," said Romanamor.

"We'd better save the potion until we need it then," said Granarg, a determined look on his face, as he marched along.

They had left the village by now and had begun the long walk across fields and through woodland, back towards the mountains, the tunnel and home.

Chapter 20

Raggar Keeps a Watch

At the tunnel entrance itself, Frogorf, Emertreme and Dortrod had tried unsuccessfully to find a way past the elves. They went back to where Raggar and the other builders were waiting.

"They are absolutely everywhere," sighed Emertreme.

"Oh dear," said Raggar. "There must be far more of them than we first thought."

"I would estimate about 150 of the evil creatures," said Frogorf.

"More than we can take on," said Raggar. "We'll just have to sit tight and see what happens."

"I think that maybe our gnome friends have been successful, otherwise why would the elves be so desperate to stop them getting here?" Said Dortrod.

"If you're right, we must keep a close watch on what the elves are up to," said Raggar.

"We'll need to post a couple of gnomes at the tunnel entrance at all times. We can't afford to miss anything."

Two of the builders were designated to keep watch over the elves and when they became tired, two more would take their place.

Chapter 21

The Walk Back to the Tunnel

For the others, the walk back towards the mountains was a long and tiring one. The younger gnomes needed to stop for a rest every now and again, and the older ones were more than grateful for an excuse to rest their weary legs.

It hadn't taken them long to get clear of the area inhabited by humans, but now they were moving to higher ground and it was uphill all the way.

"We're never going to make it back before daylight," panted Cramarc.

"I think we'll have to start looking for somewhere to hide soon."

Towards the eastern horizon the sky was already taking on the paler, blue colour, heralding the new dawn and they all agreed with Cramarc that it would be for safer to lie low for the day, then make their move toward the tunnel at night.

"There are some trees up ahead," said Tromort.

"Could be the ideal place," agreed Romanamor.

They headed towards the trees and got there just as the sun began peeping over the mountain tops. Romanamor and Tromort led them to a spot right in the middle of the trees, where they thought it would be safest. They were very tired and also very hungry by now, and once they had settled down, shared out the food that they had managed to collect on the way.

"I wonder what happened to the other gnomes we've rescued," said Tromort. "It seems strange that we haven't met any on our journey."

"I only hope that none of them have been recaptured," said Romanamor.

As if in answer to this conversation, a young gnome peered cautiously out from behind a nearby tree. He ducked in behind the tree again, then he turned round and nodded his head. Slowly more young gnomes began to appear from behind the trees and bushes, they crept slowly forward until they were stood behind the first one.

"Maybe we're going to get back home after all," the first one whispered. This particular gnome was known as Bab for short because his real name was so long, that nobody could be bothered to say it.

It was Tippit who first spotted them.

"Look over there," he said to the others. "I'm sure I saw what looked like a gnome, moving behind that tree."

"I'd better investigate. I'll try and get closer," said Granarg, getting up and walking in the direction that Tippit was looking.

Roccor and Toocoot followed Granarg just in case things weren't as they appeared to be. By the time they got there, the young gnomes had disappeared again.

"Is anybody here?" Shouted Granarg. "It's all right, we've come to help you."

One by one the gnomes came back out of hiding. Bab seemed to be the spokesgnome for the little group.

"You can't guess how pleased we are to see you," he said. "We thought we were the only ones to escape."

"There are quite a lot of us," explained Granarg. "Come and meet the others."

It was the first time that Bab and the young gnomes with him had seen Romanamor and the family since the day they were rescued. Even so, each of them recognised the gnome that had administered the potion to them.

There were lots of handshakes and vowing of eternal gratitude from the gnomes who had been saved. This went on for quite some time until Granarg interrupted.

"We must start making plans to get back to Gnomeland."

"I don't know if it's possible," said Bab. "There are an awful lot of elves between here and the tunnel."

"We've decided that we'll fight them if we have to," said Romanamor.

"Remember the potion that we gave you to turn you back into real gnomes again?"

All of the rescued gnomes nodded.

"Well, this potion also makes us braver and we've got just about enough left for everybody to have a large dose," explained Romanamor.

"What if we don't make it?" Queried Bab.

"If we don't try, we'll be stuck here forever anyway," said Roccor.

"We'll wait until darkness and make our move then, but for now, I think we ought to get some rest. We're going to need all our energy trying to get past the elves," said Granarg.

"We can keep a look out for any danger while you're sleeping," volunteered Bab.

"Thank you," said Granarg. "Be sure to wake us if anyone comes."

So the gnomes that had travelled from the village all found somewhere to rest their weary heads, and the young gnomes in the woods took up positions facing the elves' camps, ready to wake the others at the first sign of trouble.

Chapter 22

Attack of the Elves

The gnomes on guard were all aware that the elves have a very keen sense of smell and could pick up a scent from many miles away. The wind was usually blowing off the mountains, thereby wafting their scent in the opposite direction to the elves' camps. But today of all days, the wind decided to change and was slowly moving around to a position directly behind the woods. Bab had noticed the changing wind and was becoming increasingly concerned that the elves might pick up their scent, which considering the large amount of gnomes in the woods, would be very strong.

By mid-morning the wind was blowing totally in the direction of the elves' camps and as the elves were always sniffing the air with their long noses. There was no chance at all that they weren't going to pick up the scent of the gnomes.

The elves camped nearest to the woods were the first ones to catch the scent of the gnomes. Word soon got back to Snitchmire and Prodlife that there were gnomes in the vicinity.

The two leaders of the elves, closely followed by Squiggly, walked to the edge of the camp.

Noses pointed skyward, they stood still and sniffed the air.

"I'm sure the gnomes must be in those woods over there," said Snitchmire.

"Very strong scent," said Prodlife. "There must be a lot of them."

"Not enough to worry us. If we organise it properly, we could have an awful lot of solid gnomes by the end of the day," Snitchmire smiled at the thought of recapturing the gnomes.

"We'll teach them to think they can escape from us," joined in Squiggly.

Now elves, for most of the time, were very disorganised, but they were very good at planning strategies when it came to battle. They could be both organised and disciplined and they would obey their leaders without question. Between them, Snitchmire and Prodlife worked out a plan of action. It was decided that in order to prevent any gnomes escaping, they would have to surround the entire wood. With almost 200 at their disposal, Snitchmire and Prodlife were confident that their aims could easily be achieved. Once they were in position, their leaders would give a signal and the elves would all move slowly into the woods, thus making it impossible for any gnomes to escape.

"The gnomes are sure to be watching out for us," pointed out Squiggly.

"Then we shall give the woods a wide berth and approach from behind," said Prodlife, looking at Squiggly. "Now I suggest you go and round up all the elves and tell then our plan."

Soon Squiggly had collected the elves together and had given them a brief outline of what they were expected to do.

"Have you each got a pointed stick, ready to attack the gnomes?" Shouted Snitchmire.

The elves held their spindly arms in the air, holding their weapons aloft, in a typical warrior stance.

"Excellent!" Cried Snitchmire. "We'll lead the way and you lot had better be quiet, anyone who makes a sound will feel the point of my stick."

The elves moved off silently, trying their best to stay in, what was for them, a fairly neat line.

Emertreme had been watching this activity from his hiding place just inside the tunnel entrance. He rushed back to the others as quickly as he could.

"The elves seem to be leaving the camp and heading in the direction of the woods," he panted.

Raggar had been asleep but was woken up by this interruption.

"Wwwhat was that you just said?" He stammered. Emertreme repeated what he had said.

"We'd better follow them then," yawned Raggar.

"Shall we have some of the potion first?" Asked Dortrod.

"Yes, and we'd better take some with us as well," said Raggar. "You never know who else may need it."

Frogorf was pleased that his potion was being put to such good use, but now he was anxious to help in a more practical way. Raggar sensed Frogorf's urgency to follow the elves and knowing what he did about him, decided that there was no point in waiting around in the tunnel any longer.

"Come on then," he said. "Let's go and find out what the little blighters are up to."

They could tell from the direction of the smoke coming from the camp fires, that they were downwind of the elves. Whilst the wind stayed in that direction, there was a good chance that they would remain undetected.

The elves were moving quickly across the heathland towards the woods. They marched in a thin line, two or three across with Snitchmire, Prodlife and Squiggly leading the way. They were aiming at a point to the north of the woods, trying to remain unseen until such time as they had the woods completely surrounded. As they got nearer to the woods, the line of elves thinned out so that by the time they got there, they were moving in a single file, each elf a few feet behind the next one.

It was uncanny how the elves seemed to know instinctively what positions to take up around the woodland perimeter. The elves had been spotted by the young, rescued gnomes who had been on guard while the others slept. They rushed over and frantically woke everyone up.

"The elves are surrounding the woods at this very minute," said one of the young gnomes.

Granarg thought quickly.

"We can't just stay here, woods are elves' territory, we need to get out in the open."

Toocoot was already passing the last of the potion round to everybody. Cramarc and Agninga were looking particularly vulnerable at the moment, and Toocoot made sure that they had an extra-large dose of potion each.

"So which way do we go?" Asked Tromort.

"We might as well head in towards the tunnel, if we do break through that's the direction we need to go in," said Granarg.

"Let's go then, before we're completely trapped," urged Romanamor.

They were all as keen to get out as Romanamor, but which-ever direction they tried to go in, they could hear elves coming through the woods towards them.

"It's no use," cried Cramarc. "We'll never get out of here."

"Only one thing for it," said Granarg. "We must all stick very closely together and keep going in one direction, builders at the front, so that we can fight off any elves."

So with the builders leading, they marched through the woods, in the direction that they perceived to be the way home.

They hadn't been travelling for long when they came across the first of the elves. The leading builders froze when they saw the menacing look on the elves' faces and it took them a while to pluck up the courage to say anything.

"You will move out of the way and let us pass," growled Granarg.

"Not a chance, you stupid, old gnome," hissed one of the elves. "You might as well give up now."

"No! This time the gnomes are not going to give in!" Shouted Granarg, walking towards the elves, closely followed by Toocoot, Roccor and the other builders.

The elves were totally taken aback by the aggressive attitude of the gnomes. They were only used to gnomes being timid. The gnomes took advantage of the surprise they had caused and charged their way through. A few of the gnomes got jabbed with the pointed sticks, but they managed to break through the line of elves, virtually unscathed. Word of what had happened, spread like wildfire around the circle of elves, who all began moving as fast as they could, towards the point where the gnomes had broken through their ranks. As the elves could move much faster than the gnomes, it wasn't long before they had caught up with and surrounded them.

"And where do you think you're going?" Shouted Snitchmire.

"Home!" Granarg shouted back.

"Wrong," hissed Snitchmire. "Home is the last place that you're going."

The elves cackled when Snitchmire said this.

The gnomes were starting to feel scared now, a quick calculation told Granarg, that there must be nearly 150 elves and even he was beginning to feel afraid.

"We're not giving up without a fight," he stammered.

"Come on then gnome, do your worst," said Squiggly, shaking his pointed stick.

Granarg and the other builders plucked up every ounce of courage that they possessed and charged at the elves. Romanamor, Tromort and a few of the rescued gnomes joined in the fray. Some of the builders were using sticks that they'd found whilst they were in the woods, but they were untrained in the art of battle, and the elves were very quick. There was the occasional cry of pain as one of the sticks hit a target. Some of the builders managed to disarm a few elves and use their own weapons against them, but slowly and inevitably, the elves were overcoming the gnomes. Despite the potion, some of the young gnomes had become solid again and had to be carried, which slowed down the gnomes even more. There was an awful situation, where Cramarc became separated from the others and found herself surrounded by a group of vicious elves. They stabbed at her with their pointed sticks and she was so terrified that she went solid on the spot. Romanamor and one or two others battled through to try and save her but they were too late.

"Ho ym, ho ym," wailed Romanamor, picking up his solidified wife.

"Tahw era ew gniog ot od?" He quickly looked around to make sure that Pullup, Tippit and Potstop were still moving. He looked pleadingly at the elves, but there was no sign of any mercy, in fact the elves were grinning, it was a long time since they had enjoyed themselves as much as this.

The elves were slowly moving the gnomes back towards the woods and once inside, intended to keep on scaring them until every last one had gone solid. Snitchmire and Prodlife were standing to one side, enjoying every minute of their victory.

"The Duke and Duchess are going to be very proud of what we've achieved today," said Prodlife.

"We should be well rewarded when we get back home," agreed Snitchmire.

Romanamor looked across at them, how he'd love to wipe those smug grins off their stupid, pointy faces. Alas there was nothing that or any of the others could do.

The elves were still self-congratulating themselves, when help for the gnomes came out of nowhere.

Chapter 23

The Final Conflict

THERE WERE SOME LARGE BOULDERS between the woods and the elves' campsite, behind which, Raggar, Frogorf and the 28 builders with them, had been hiding and watching the proceedings. They were timing their attack for when they thought the elves would be least expecting it and now seemed to be the right time. They were quite a distance away from the elves, but the roar they let out as they began charging towards them could easily be heard. This was a very angry band of gnomes, all fortified with large doses of Frogorf's potion.

As we know, warfare and aggressiveness doesn't come naturally to gnomes, and they had spent a long time working themselves up for this assault. They had picked up various weapons along the way, some had found large sticks and others had found small rocks, all very useful for clobbering elves with.

The gnomes were secretly hoping that their mad charge would be enough to frighten the elves away and they wouldn't have to use the weapons, which was why they were making as much noise as they possibly could. In a way they were right; the elves were taken completely by surprise, but instead of running away, they stood still and just stared at the oncoming builders. Seeing that the elves were distracted, Granarg, Toocoot, Roccor and the other builders attacked them from behind and grabbed as many of their pointed sticks as possible. The closer Frogorf got, the clearer the elves could see his bulging muscles and the contorted look of anger on his face. He had waited 180 years for a chance to get his revenge on the elves for what they had done to his family. The crazy mood of Frogorf was contagious and the others were all as angry as he was. They crashed into the first line of elves and began lashing out with their weapons. The elves were not used to violence being directed at them; they were far more used to dishing it out. They were actually struggling to fight back, more and more of them were thinking better of getting involved and were backing off. Granarg and the others were doing very well and although most of them had been stabbed a few times, none of them had sustained any more than superficial wounds. However, the damage inflicted on the elves was not so superficial.

There were a lot of elves' bodies strewn around. Some were just temporarily dazed but some had wounds of a far more serious nature. A lot of the elves would die where they lay, others were just capable of crawling off into the woods to recover.

The gnomes had never killed anyone or anything in their lives before, but now was not the time to sit and ponder what they had done. There were still an awful lot of elves to deal with, and the gnomes were totally preoccupied with trying to overcome them.

Some of the gnomes had become cut off from the rest and were surrounded by elves, which were stabbing mercilessly at them with their pointed sticks. Frogorf noticed the plight of these gnomes and letting out a huge roar, charged towards them and began belting elves left, right and centre. The elves scattered like frightened mice and the gnomes who had been in trouble were able to join the others. Some of these unfortunate gnomes had been very badly injured, after being stabbed several times, mostly in the neck, and they were very glad of Frogorf's timely intervention.

Snitchmire and Prodlife realised that the gnomes were getting the upper hand and began a slow retreat, towards the safety of the woods. Other elves joined them and soon they were all headed towards the woods.

Chapter 24

The Journey Home

When the gnomes saw that the elves were giving up, they began moving in the direction of the tunnel, their progress slowed down because they had to carry the gnomes who had gone solid. To their horror, they realised that some of the gnomes weren't just solid but had died from the stab wounds inflicted by the elves. These gnomes had died heroes and it was decided that they must be taken with them and given an honourable burial when they got back to Gnomeland.

Romanamor was exhausted after the battle and didn't have the strength to carry the now solidified Cramarc. One of the builders picked her up and gently put her across his broad shoulders. Romanamor thanked him.

"Don't worry," said the builder. "We have plenty of potion back in the tunnel."

Snitchmire and Prodlife were desperately trying to regroup the elves into some sort of attacking force.

"You're nothing more than a bunch of snivelling cowards," ranted Snitchmire.

"How can we show our faces in Elfland after what's happened?" Wailed Prodlife.

"We need to recapture those gnomes," said Snitchmire, looking frantically round for elves that might look brave enough to try. The elves all looked away, ashamed of the fact that they were too scared to try and attack the gnomes again.

The young gnomes were in a state of euphoria. Just a couple of days ago they were garden ornaments and were either sitting, standing or lying in one position, and now they were alive again and heading back home. Some of them had been in Humanland for so long that they weren't sure if their families would even be alive, when they got back to Gnomeland.

Frogorf unfortunately never found any of his family; the humans had probably taken them out of the area. It was in the back of his mind to return one day and search further into Humanland to try and find them. Despite not finding them, he had lost his feeling of guilt that had stayed with him through the years. After all, his potion had worked and he had come back to help all these other gnomes. He was now a hero and it balanced out the fact that he was a coward all those years ago.

Pullup, Tippit and Potstop were very upset about their mother being solid, but they knew that when they got back to where the potion was, everything would be all right again. They walked proudly alongside their father, for he was the one who had instigated the rescue and without him, nothing would have ever been done. The kind builder who was carrying Cramarc was also walking just behind the little family group. Naggan was delighted to be reunited with his parents and they with him.

Pingnip meanwhile, had joined up with the other young gnomes who had been in the same garden as him. For they had become friends over the years, despite the fact that they had been solid.

Toocoot and Roccor were leading the way back, but most of the other builders were bringing up the rear just in case the elves decided to attack again.

They were walking through the elves' camps now, which as you can imagine, were an utter shambles. Around most of the campsites there were the remains of dead squirrels or rats that had been partially eaten by the elves. This sight was quite abhorrent to the gnomes and many of them had to avert their gaze before it made them sick. Soon they were in sight of the entrance to the cave system that would take them home again. The actual entrance was well hidden by the prickly shrubbery that had been planted by the elves, but even so, they caught occasional glimpses of it as they approached. They were a little apprehensive as they neared the tunnel because for all they knew, there might still be some elves hanging around the entrance. Fortunately, the elves had been so confident of their ability to capture the gnomes, that they had all gone with Snitchmire and Prodlife to the woods.

It was nightfall as they entered the tunnel. They searched around for the torches that had been left there by Romanamor, but alas, they were no longer there.

"Probably stolen by the elves," said Romanamor.

"More than likely," agreed Raggar. "We'll have to travel the first bit in complete darkness when we get to the cave that we hid in, we can pick up the extra potion that we left there. Were there any torches left?"

"I think there may have been one left," answered Dortrod.

"Better than none at all," said Raggar.

The gnomes had become quite used to travelling at night and were not unduly worried about being in the dark tunnel. Nevertheless there was the occasional cry of, "Ouch!" As one of the gnomes bumped into the rough sides.

"Ah," said Raggar. "I think we're at the cave where we left the potion and the torch, if you'll just wait here, I'll see if I can find them."

Raggar decided to go in alone, he couldn't risk everyone going in as it would be too easy for one of them to upset the precious flagons of potion. He groped carefully round in the dark for a while before he found the torch. He took two flints from the small bag that he always carried on his shoulder and struck them together near the top of the torch, eventually succeeding in lighting it. It may have only been one torch, but the glow from it, lit up the whole cave.

There were three flagons of potion over by the far wall and three of the builders came in and picked them up. It was decided to leave the cart where it was for the time being as pushing it would only slow them down.

They continued on through the tunnel at a faster pace because now they could see where they were going. Unfortunately the torch, although very bright, didn't last very long and the gnomes were soon in darkness once again. Because of the darkness, it took them longer to travel through the tunnel than any of them had taken coming the other way. They didn't dare stop for a break in case the elves caught up with them and it seemed to them as if they were walking forever. The builder carrying Cramarc had become very weary and another builder had taken over the task. They had decided not to use the potion on the solid gnomes just yet as reviving them would take up some of their precious travelling time.

They travelled through the first night, then through the next day and all through the second night and each gnome was now, mechanically putting one leg in front of the other, forcing themselves forwards towards their goal. It was early the next morning before they could see any sign that they were reaching the other end. The complete blackness of the tunnel slowly changed to a darkish, murky grey and then progressively the grey became lighter until finally the gnomes at the front of the line could see the small circle of light that heralded the end of the tunnel.

The gnomes sub-consciously sped up when they saw that the exit was getting nearer. The gnomes at the back of the line could not see the exit, but they began walking faster to keep up with the gnomes in front.

It was a dull, damp day when they finally emerged into Gnomeland, but to the gnomes, it was a glorious day. To Romanamor, Tippit, Pullup, Potstop, Tromort, Agninga and Naggan it was the most ecstatic day of their whole lives. They danced around in the rain, the aches and pains of their effort, completely forgotten. Granarg was trying to get some kind of normality back to the proceedings.

"Look," He said. "We're not even going to be able to get as far as Grassroot unless we rest for a while. But first I suggest we use the potion to revive the solid gnomes."

The dancing stopped when Granarg mentioned reviving the solid gnomes. Romanamor looked across at Cramarc.

"There's nothing I want more than to see her moving around again."

"Right let's do it then!" Said Granarg.

The rain had stopped for a while, which was probably just as well, because the flagons containing the potion were open to the elements. The solid gnomes were tipped onto their backs and the potion was poured into their slightly open mouths. Slowly they came back into the land of the living, their eyes began to come back into focus again and it was with relief that they saw they were surrounded by gnomes.

Cramarc looked up at Romanamor and smiled a knowing grin. Romanamor looked lovingly down at her. "It's good to have you back," he said.

"It's wonderful to be back," she replied.

"Are we really back in Gnomeland?" Asked one of the newly recovered young gnomes.

"Of course you are," said Tromort. "And hopefully, this time you'll stay here."

Many of the gnomes were overcome with emotion, some of them were openly weeping, partly with joy but mostly with the relief of returning home. In their darkest moments in Humanland, they had truly believed that they would never again return.

Romanamor and Tromort were going round shaking the hands of all the builders who had come to their rescue. They thanked Frogorf profusely, for without his crazy charge into the midst of the elves, they may well have lost the battle. Also, without Frogorf's potion, there would not have been an expedition in the first place.

"We'd like you to come and live with us in Grassroot," said Romanamor.

"I thank you for the kind offer, but I think I'd rather return to my cave. I've got used to being on my own, but I promise to come and visit you as often as I can," said Frogorf.

"Well, you are most welcome at any time," said Romanamor, sincerely.

The adrenaline, or potion, or whatever it was that had kept the gnomes going, was beginning to wear off now and most of them had fallen asleep. Eventually the only gnomes still awake were the ones who had been recently revived. Cramarc sat talking to the young gnomes, whilst at the same time keeping an eye on the tunnel, in case any elves should appear.

A couple of hours rest and the gnomes were awake and ready to make their move back to Grassroot. It was decided to travel back around the northern edge of the lake because to go the other way would mean crossing the river that the gnomes had a problem crossing on their outward journey. After the rain, the river would be swollen, making it impassable, even to the builders. They reached the lake soon after setting off. The walk around it would be a long one, but because they knew that Grassroot was on the other side, it would not be tedious.

During the march, the builders discussed what was to be done about the elves.

"They are definitely going to try and return to Elfland," said Granarg.

"Agreed," said Raggar. "But it's up to us to make sure they go straight back there, without causing any mischief."

"We are going to need as many volunteers as possible to shepherd them through; we'll have to organise it as soon as we get to Grassroot," said Granarg.

Chapter 25

Rerurn to Grassroot

The downside to their happy return was the fact that some gnomes had actually been killed in the battle. There were five altogether; four builders and one of the young gnomes who had been rescued. The builders took it in turns to carry the bodies; the dead builders were heavy, but the gnomes were determined to give them a decent burial when they got back to Stonemarble. There was a place, sacred to the gnomes, just to the north of the town. Gnomes had been buried here for centuries and this is where the bodies of the dead heroes were being taken.

It was a few hours before the gnomes saw any sign that they were getting near to Grassroot. The first indication was the plumes of smoke rising from the cooking fires, a heavenly sight indeed to Romanamor and his family, for they knew that they would soon be back among their friends and neighbours once more.

Slowly, the village itself came into view and for the weary gnomes it was a very welcome sight indeed. At the first cottage they came to, there was an old gnome in the garden. He was concentrating on hoeing a row of carrots and at first he didn't even look up, then something in him sensed that he was being watched, he turned round slowly and was greeted by the amazing sight of over 80 gnomes, trudging along the pathway, next to his cottage.

"Well I'll be a crumpled, carrot cruncher!" He exclaimed. "Is it really you?"

"Yes, it's really us," Romanamor shouted back.

The old gnome was a bit stuck as to what to say next, finally he said, "I must tell the others," and rushed into the cottage as fast as his old legs would carry him. A few seconds later, the whole family emerged, waving and cheering. Two of the younger gnomes ran to the next cottage and told the occupants the good news. The gnomes in the next cottage did the same and very soon the news of the adventurers' return had spread, like wildfire, throughout the whole village. By the time they had reached the main street, the whole population of Grassroot had come out to welcome them. The sides of the main street were thick with cheering and waving gnomes.

The returning gnomes were totally taken aback by the reception, but they carried on marching nevertheless. Some parent gnomes were looking anxiously at the young, rescued gnomes in the parade, trying to see if their young, kidnapped children were amongst them. Conversely, the young gnomes were looking across trying to see if they recognised their parents. A lot of very happy reunions were taking place.

The majority of kidnapped gnomes had been taken from Grassroot, as the elves were usually too lazy to carry them all the way from Stonemarble. Any gnomes who had been taken from Stonemarble would travel back with the builders after a good night's rest.

Gnong was quite breathless when he arrived at the main street, he had got there as fast as his stumpy, old legs could carry him, but he was still one of the last gnomes to arrive. Everyone in the village knew him and the throng of gnomes parted so that he could go through to the front. Gnong was very grateful to the gnomes who had let him through and thanked them as he squeezed past. The procession of gnomes walking down the main street were almost at the point where Gnong was stood anxiously waiting. He looked along the line of homecomers and could just make out the heads of Romanamor and Cramarc halfway along. Without further ado, he rushed forward to greet them. First, he gave Cramarc a great big hug and then he shook Romanamor firmly by the hand. He looked across at the children, not believing his eyes. One, two, three he counted, over and over again. "Potstop, is that really you, or are my old eyes playing tricks?"

"Yes Uncle," replied Potstop. "It's really me and I can scarcely believe that I'm here myself."

Gnong bent over and picked Potstop up in his strong arms, forgetting at the time, about his weak back. "Ouch," he exclaimed, putting Potstop down and clenching the small of his back. After years and years of digging, a lot of gnomes end up with bad backs and Gnong was no exception.

The others weren't sure whether to sympathise or laugh at the almost comical expression on Gnong's face.

"That'll teach me," he cursed. "But it was worth it, to hold Potstop in my arms once again."

Everyone went all gooey and emotional at this point, until Romanamor broke the moment. "Come on," he said. "Let's catch up with the others."

The army of returning gnomes were all heading for the communal hut in the centre of the village. The villagers had been preparing for this moment, even though they weren't certain if the adventuring gnomes would ever return. By the time they reached the communal hut, everything was set up. There was a huge, *Welcome Home* banner across the top of the doorway and inside, various villagers were busy preparing some of the gnomes' favourite food. At the far end of the hut sat the elders of the village. They stood up when the returning gnomes entered, out of respect for what they had achieved.

Eventually all of the gnomes had managed to crowd into the hut. Corabaroc, the chief elder, cleared his throat ready to make a speech. The hut fell silent waiting to hear what he had to say. Finally he felt ready to start speaking.

"First of all," he said. "I'd like to say just how overjoyed we all are to see you again. We've had our doubts whether you would ever get back here safely. Secondly, I'd like to congratulate you on your great, nay, monumental achievement and thirdly I'd like to thank you on behalf of all the families involved, for rescuing so many of their little ones."

He paused for breath and to collect his thoughts. "Now I'm sure that all you want to do is get some sleep, but first, we'd be honoured if you would stay for a while and partake of some food and ale. There's carrot juice and apple juice for the young ones."

"Three cheers for Romanamor," said Martram. "Hip hip! Hooray! Hip hip! Hooray! Hip hip! Hooray!"

Romanamor was rather embarrassed by this adulation, but deep down, he was proud of what he had achieved. It was just beginning to sink in that he, an ordinary, hard-working gnome had managed to rescue so many kidnapped gnomes from Humanland. If the elves had carried on kidnapping at the same rate, very soon there would have been no young gnomes left at all, and without young gnomes, the whole future of the race would have been in jeopardy.

The villagers had provided some chairs so that everyone in the hut could sit down whilst they were eating. Soon the only sounds to be heard, were the appreciative grunts of the hungry gnomes and the occasional loud slurp when they took a mouthful of drink.

Gnong sat with the elders who were discussing the best course of action to take regarding the elves.

"Shame we can't keep them in Humanland," grumbled Wollow. "They'd never trouble us again."

"I've been thinking of a way that we can stop them coming back, if we get them safely through to Elfland," said Martram.

"And did you reach any conclusion?" Asked Corabaroc.

"Yes, I did," replied Martram. "All we have to do is to get the builders to build some sort of wall across the tunnel entrance into Elfland. If it doesn't stop them altogether, at least it should keep them at bay for a good, long time."

"So simple, it's brilliant!" Exclaimed Barrab. "I'm surprised one of us didn't think of it before."

"We'll arrange to get the wall built as soon as the elves are all back in Elfland," said Corabaroc.

The builders were already discussing how to go about shepherding the elves back through Gnomeland. There was a sense of urgency, because the elves could come through at any time and something had to be organised quickly.

"We need gnomes at the north end of the lake right away, so that we can direct them on a path well clear of Grassroot," said Granarg.

"There isn't time to get help from Stonemarble; we'll have to use the gnomes that are already here," said Roccor.

"Volunteers are what we need, and volunteers are what we shall get," said a determined Corabaroc.

Word soon got around that they were looking for volunteers and almost every gnome in the village wanted to take part in the great herding of the elves. In the end nearly 300 gnomes willing to help had volunteered. More than enough, thought Corabaroc, to make sure the blighters don't cause any trouble.

The adventuring gnome heroes had finished eating and were now feeling very sleepy indeed. Romanamor and Cramarc looked at their three very tired offspring and decided it would be all right to make their excuses and leave. Romanamor invited Tromort to do the same. "You can stay with us for a while and when the elves are all back where they belong, I'm sure some of the gnomes will help us to build you a hut of your own in the village."

"Are you sure that you've got room?" Asked Tromort.

"Of course we have, Uncle Gnong can move in with us, I'm positive that he won't mind and you can use his rooms in the annex," said Romanamor.

"Very kind of you, old friend. I'm sure that we're going to enjoy living in Grassroot again," said a grateful Tromort.

"We still have quite a few belongings back in our old hut," said Agninga.

"Don't worry," said Tromort. "There will be plenty of time to fetch them later on."

Naggan had fallen asleep in his chair at such an angle that he was nearly falling off it. Rather than wake him up, Tromort decided that it would be far kinder to carry him. Pullup, Tippit and Potstop were also very weary, but they were determined to make it home under their own steam. Everyone wanted to shake their hands as they left and it took them quite a while to get out into the open air.

The hut was situated at the other end of the village and it was a long, slow walk for the tired gnomes.

"My home," exclaimed Cramarc.

"I never thought I'd see it again."

"Neither did we," said Pullup and Tippit in unison.

"And I didn't either," sighed Potstop.

"I always had faith that we would get back here," said Romanamor.

"It was only the thought of coming back that kept me going."

Some of the neighbours were already back in their huts. One of them kindly lent Tromort a bed for Naggan to use, as all three gnomes were not going to fit into Gnong's bed. They were completely exhausted and it wasn't long before the hut reverberated with the sound of snoring once again.

Chapter 26

Shepherding the Elves

Back in Humanland, Snitchmire and Prodlife had been trying to concoct a story that would exonerate them from any blame for what had happened. They thought as hard as they could, but couldn't reach any conclusion, other than the fact that they, as the elves in charge, would have to accept the consequences when they returned home. They decided to try and retrieve the situation by making as much trouble as possible on their journey back through Gnomeland. Little did they know about the army of gnomes that were waiting, to make sure, that they went quietly, through gnome territory. The elves were very despondent after their defeat by the gnomes, but they cheered up a bit, now that Snitchmire and Prodlife had suggested causing mischief. They were getting more and more excited as they walked through the tunnel.

When they emerged from the other end and headed for the lake, they were still chattering away about the kind of things that they were going to do.

"We can set fire to the gnomes' huts," said one.

"Maybe burn the whole village," said another.

"They'll all run out and go solid again," sniggered a third.

"They will know the true meaning of a pointed stick," said the first one.

"Yeah! Jab, jab, jab!" Another one joined in, pretending to stab at imaginary gnomes.

"Oi! Watch what you're doing with that thing," shouted the elf directly in front of the one doing the jabbing.

The elves were becoming more confident as they walked towards the lake, and they were totally unaware of the gnomes that had gathered just around the top corner. The elves almost bumped into the waiting gnomes before they realised what was happening. Three hundred or so very determined-looking gnomes, all armed with various garden implements, were blocking the way. Male, female and young gnomes had all volunteered to make sure the elves behaved themselves. Granarg, Raggar and some of the older builders were too worn out to take part, but Toocoot, Roccor, Emertreme and Dortrod, plus some of the younger builders were all there. At their head was the indomitable figure of Frogorf.

"Stop right where you are!" He boomed. "Drop your weapons and you won't get hurt!"

There was a time lapse, whilst the elves weighed up whether it would be worth fighting or not. They remembered the manner in which they had been defeated by the builders in Humanland and, being basically cowards, decided to drop their pointed sticks.

There were clatters, as one by one, the weapons were thrown to the ground.

"Good!" Bellowed Frogorf. "Now all walk forward until you are well clear of the pointed sticks."

The elves did so.

"And now you will form an orderly line," said Frogorf, beginning to enjoy himself.

The elves did as they were told. Then the gnomes formed a line alongside the elves, so that they couldn't possibly move towards Grassroot.

"Right, march!" Shouted Frogorf.

The elves began a slow, reluctant march back to Elfland and even Snitchmire and Prodlife realised that there was no point in arguing.

A messenger had been sent to Stonemarble with the purpose of collecting together as many volunteers as possible to take over from the others, at some point between Grassroot and Stonemarble.

It would be a couple of days before the elves were all safely back home, but the gnomes made it impossible for them to get up to any of their tricks. An even greater number of volunteers came out from Stonemarble to take over from the others at the allotted point halfway between the two places.

When these volunteers had taken over, the gnomes returned to Grassroot. The villagers had found enough beds for all the builders and set them up in the communal hut. Some of them had given up their own beds, so that these visitors would have somewhere comfortable to sleep. A small price to pay after what these builders had done for them. When the builders returned, they all collapsed gratefully onto the beds and nothing or nobody was going to wake them up until they were ready.

The elves had been awake for as long as the gnomes, but the Stonemarble volunteers were determined not to let them rest and it was a very tired, dejected group of elves who finally arrived at the tunnel entrance leading to Elfland. Once the elves were safely inside the caves, most of the volunteers returned to Stonemarble. A few stayed behind to make sure the elves didn't try to get back out, although there was not much chance of this happening, as the elves had given up any thoughts of revenge for the time being. It was a very sad looking army of elves who finally emerged into Elfland. Snitchmire decided that they all needed a good, long rest before they went anywhere near the main town of Pointstick. They were also going to need a long time to collect their thoughts before they faced the wrath of the Duke and Duchess.

When they thought that they had rested for long enough and had plucked up enough courage, they made their move towards Pointstick. It wasn't far and they arrived there in just over an hour. The Duke and Duchess had been forewarned of their approach and were awaiting them with open arms. Until, that is, they saw the dejected look on the elves' faces. They knew immediately that something was wrong and asked Snitchmire what had happened. Snitchmire spoke very slowly, as if the longer he took to say it, the more time he would have to think of excuses. In the end he had told the Duke and Duchess everything that had gone on.

The Duke flew into a rage. "You are the most useless elves in the whole land!" He screamed at Snitchmire and Prodlife. "Because of your incompetence, we've lost our entire trade with the humans!" He flung his arms up in despair. "No more fiery liquid!" He exclaimed.

"No more beautiful jewels," cried the Duchess.

"No more meat, no more whatever else it is that we get," wailed the Duke.

"No more jewels," repeated the Duchess.

"Sorry," said Snitchmire and Prodlife together.

"Sorry? I'll give you sorry!" Shouted the Duke. "I'll make you very sorry indeed that you couldn't overcome a few useless gnomes."

"There wasn't a few, and they weren't useless," said Prodlife. "That potion they had seemed to make them stronger."

"Well no matter how many, or how strong the potion was, I would still expect the elves to win," shrieked the Duke. "What's to be done with them?"

He looked across at the Duchess. In fact they all looked at the Duchess, who had an evil grin, on her pointed face.

"Well," she said finally. "For such treachery as you have committed, the normal penalty would be death by pointed stick, but as you are our only children, we shall be a bit more lenient." She looked at the Duke for approval, he nodded, then she went on.

"I thought maybe a few months' hard labour in the fields would make you sorry."

"Oh no mother, please, anything else but that!" Pleaded Snitchmire, who had never done a days' work in his life.

"It's decided," said the Duke. "And it's final!"

The elves get most of their food by stealing from the gnomes, however they do grow some of their own vegetables, but all the work is done by elves that have upset the Duke and Duchess. It was considered to be a very bad punishment indeed as the vegetable fields were organised by very hard taskmasters. They made the elves in their charge work solidly, from sunrise to sunset.

The Duke made sure that no favouritism would be shown to his sons, in fact he told the taskmaster to be harder on them, than he was on the rest.

"That should teach them a lesson," he said to the Duchess.

"I don't think they'll let us down again in a hurry," she replied, still grinning.

"And now the rest of you will go back and show these gnomes just how nasty elves can really be," sneered the Duke. "Now be off with you, or it'll be death for everyone."

The elves very reluctantly turned round and began heading back towards the tunnel. They wondered what they could do to retrieve the situation, but they knew it would be almost certain death if they failed.

Meanwhile in Stonemarble, the elders had called an emergency meeting. They had decided that it was time to stop the elves from coming through, once and for all. Blocking the entrance to the tunnel was the only way to successfully do this and the 10 or so builders who remained in Stonemarble were summoned to the meeting. The elders explained what was required of them and they went off immediately to begin loading building blocks onto their carts. Some ordinary gnomes went with them to act as labourers, whilst the builders did the actual building. They thought that four cartloads would be enough for the time being, plus a large quantity of the muddy stuff, that they used to join the blocks together.

It wasn't far to the tunnel entrance from Stonemarble and they were soon hard at work. They worked faster than they had ever done in their lives; they needed to in case the elves came. The ordinary gnomes handed the blocks to the builders and as fast as they could do this, the builders made the wall. They decided that a double thick wall would be far more secure, which meant building one wall and then building another, directly in front of it. It was just as they had finished the first wall that they heard the elves coming through the tunnel on the other side. These elves, who had been ordered back by the Duke and Duchess, found themselves confronted by the large wall. The gnomes could hear the cries of despair and anguish coming from the other side, but it only strengthened their resolve to build the second wall in double quick time.

Both walls were now completed and the sound of the elves was much fainter, but the builders could still hear the chink, chink noise as the elves used stones to try and break through the wall.

"It'll take them forever," said one of the builders. "But if they succeed, we'll build it back up again."

Satisfied that they had done a good job, the builders went back to Stonemarble for a well-earned meal.

The elves, who were too scared to go back and face the Duke and Duchess, carried on chinking away at the wall. They would break through eventually, but as the gnomes thought, it would take them a very long time indeed.

Conclusion

Life in Grassroot was slowly getting back to normal. The builders had said their farewells and made their way back to Stonemarble. Frogorf had returned to his cave up beyond the Grey Wood and the other adventurers had gone back to working on their vegetable plots. The gnomes in Grassroot had all mucked in to build a hut for Tromort, Agninga and Naggan to live in, for which they were very grateful. Tromort went up to his old home, along with Romanamor and a couple of other gnomes, to collect all the family's personal belongings. Gnomes get very attached to their gardening and cooking implements and the new hut wouldn't seem like home without them.

On the first Saturday night after Romanamor and company returned, it was decided to throw a big party involving everyone in the village. They had such a good time that it was agreed to have such a party every couple of months.

On the Sunday morning following the party, it was a really sunny day and Romanamor was up early, sitting on a chair outside his hut.

Only now was it beginning to sink in that they were finally home and everything was back to normal. They heard that the exit from the elves' tunnel had been successfully blocked, which meant that they could relax now, for the first time in Romanamor's long memory.

Gnong joined Romanamor at the front of the hut, puffing on his cherrywood pipe.

"Beautiful day," he said.

"Yes, it is," agreed Romanamor. "A beautiful, peaceful day."

www.ingramcontent.com/pod-product-compliance
Lightning Source LLC
LaVergne TN
LVHW041629060526
838200LV00040B/1510
9781739181208